The Broken Badge
The Legend of Sam Cooper

D. F. Sparks

The Broken Badge
The Legend of Sam Cooper
Copyright © 2020 by D. F. Sparks

Library of Congress Control Number: 2020922168
ISBN-13: Paperback: 978-1-64749-271-7
           ePub: 978-1-64749-272-4

Printed in the United States of America

GoToPublish LLC
1-888-337-1724
www.gotopublish.com
info@gotopublish.com

CONTENTS

PRELUDE

Samuel Cooper, A former Texas Ranger turned United States marshal. A highly religious man and a firm believer in reincarnation, the afterlife, heaven, hell, the devil, and most of all, "God". Had dedicated his life to upholding the law and defending the innocent when his parents were killed by a gang of marauders, he set out on a personal journey to bring every one of these men before the bar, to answer for the blood they had shed, and the innocent lives they had destroyed. The leader of this gang goes by the name of Klein, A cold-blooded killer who feels nothing for anybody or anything. After a long pursuit Cooper is finally captured by the notorious outlaw and with his dying breath, he places a curse on the outlaw and swears that another will wear his badge and will come for him. When he does, hell will be in his right hand in the form of a colt 45. This is the story from the start to finish at the legend of the broken badge. Maybe right doesn't always win, but it always makes a strong statement and brings forth a judgment either in this life or the next.

CHAPTER 1

Being tied to a tree and knowing that you are going to die, makes your mind do funny things. They have said that your life flashes before your eyes when you are about to die. After having been severely beaten by the Klein gang, US Marshal, Samuel Cooper had been tied to a tree and used for target practice. So as he was slowly but surely bleeding to death, he cursed the Klein gang by saying "There will be another who will take my place and he will bring you down! This cursed I placed on you, Alan Choctaw Kline." Then with the last of the strength that he had in his body. He started to remember places that he had seen , things he had done , and people he had known , all in all it didn't seem that he had lived too bad of a life. The one constellation was going to be, his death would be avenged. Samuel James Cooper was born on a small farm just south of Little Rock, Arkansas, to Emmit and Catherine Cooper, on 14 February in the year of our Lord 1843. He was the youngest of three boys. The oldest being Roy, then Leon, then there was a sister, Dorothy, Who was only one year old when Samuel Cooper began. The family had decided to move from Arkansas to East Texas when Samuel was about six months old. Emmit Cooper had been a sharecropper for most of his life and he had been told of land in Texas that could be homesteaded, so he picked up his family and headed west with hope of a new and more productive life. They travelled till they found land suitable to them. The two older boys were expected to do the chores, boys were expected to do the chores around the house and the girl was expected to help her mama with the cooking, laundry and cleaning of the house. In the evening his mother would school them for a couple of hours each night. This is the way he learned to read and to write. As Samuel had grown so had his yearned for adventure, His brothers on the other hand were quite satisfied helping their father farm their own land, instead of someone else's. His sister Dorothy had met and married a young man from Nacogdoches and had moved to the settlement, which at the time was very small. There was a train depot, a general store, with a post office inside. A stage stop, and of course, as a saloon and the livery stable. There Was a Texas Ranger that used to come by the farm every six to eight weeks and visit. He would tell Sam's mom and dad about all the things that Were happening back east, and further west, he would talk about the rampaging Indians, and where they had last struck. from time to time he would bring news of clashes between the cavalry and Indians got closer and closer , until one day the rangers suggested to Mr. cooper that he pack up his family and move closer to Nacogdoches, he said that being out in the prairie alone, especially with a family was not the safest thing he could do . He asked for the safety of his own family that they move at once. Samuel's dad and mom said no, this was their land and they would protect it to their last breath. Sam Cooper had grown into a strong , hard young man by the age of 16 .His father had taught him how to use a rifle and a side arm , he had taught him , with the help of the Texas ranger , to track . Sam had become very proficient in his accuracy with a rifle and there were a few men who could match him in speed with his sidearm. Then one day Matt had been sent into Nacogdoches for supplies. His father had decided he was going to fence in about one acre on both sides of the small stream that runs through his property, so he could raise some pigs. He also wanted to build an area that he could use to help wean young calves from their mothers. Emmett Cooper Had become known for his ability to raise extremely good quality beef cattle, and He also raised milk cows. The beef cattle was a mix between a Herford and a Texas Longhorn, the Milk cows he had brought with him from Arkansas, they were Holstein. The Milk cows produced in the vicinity of three gallon of milk per day, of which 1 gallon a day from each cow would go to the general store in Nacogdoches, usually took all day. So it was almost dark when he got to the edge of his father's property and had seen the home that he was raised in, burning. Spurring the team of horses into a dead run and pulling them up a good distance from the house. he's seen a band of men going through his family's belongings that had been thrown out of the burning house , he also seen the bodies of his father , his mother and his two brothers lying in the front yard , he stood watching as a man mounted and rode away . All the next day Sam spent digging graves, He buried each one with extreme gentleness and care. He dug a grave for his mom and dad wide enough that they could be laid side by side and holding hands. His brothers were laid on each side, Roy the oldest was laid next to his father, Leon was laid next to his mother. Sam then found some lumber And a saw and made four crosses. He Then found a small file, built a fire to heat up the file and burnt their names and the day they died on the cross. Then Sam sat down on the ground next to the graves, and cried. Sam was still sitting on the ground the next day when the Texas Ranger rode up. Seeing what had happened the ranger told Sam to saddle himself a Horse and if any of the things hanging on the line outback was his, get them and put them in his saddle bags and come with him. The ranger's name was Ben Johnson, he was well known for his exploits against the outlaws that seemed to roam free and Texas and the badlands of the Oklahoma territory. He took Sam under his wing and got him into the rangers and assigned as his partner and this is how the legend of Sam cooper be gone. for the next couple of years Sam became very efficient at being a law men, But he never forgot the name that he had heard that night, "Choctaw" Was what one of the men had called the leader of the bunch of men that had murdered his family and he had vowed that sooner or later he would come across this man and his gang. There would be no quarter given, one or the other, either Sam or this man called Choctaw Would die, the first time they laid eyes on each other would be the last time. It was a sunny spring day when Johnson sent word that he wanted to see Sam in his office at ranger's headquarters. Figuring that it was another case for him and Johnson, he had voted it back to the compound. Sam had been on leave for two days, resting up from the last case that he and Johnson was on. There had been a lot of gunplay And Sam had been wounded in his left leg not seriously, but enough to keep him off of a horse for a few days. The doctor had cleared him to go back to work, but had also said that a couple more days rest wouldn't hurt. When Sam walked into Johnson's office, he was all hyped up, looking forward to getting back to work. Johnson Motioned for Sam to sit down and then he said , "Sam , it's time that you go out on your own , there isn't any More that I can teach you, now is the time for you to make a name of your own . There is a little town that sets on the Texas line and the New Mexico territory. The town is called El Paso and you are being assigned a post there. So pack your things, horse, and all, and get to the train station." Then Johnson stood up, stuck out his hand, "You have learned well Sam, you have everything you need to become a well-known Texas Ranger. So I don't need to tell you to take your time, pick up the spots that favor you before you do anything, and keep your back to the wind, the sun to your back and your eyes forward and your temper in check. Goodbye my friend, I shall never forget you."! Sam walked out onto the porch and stood there looking around, he was quite sure that a lot of these rangers that he was looking at, he would never see again. So he wanted to remember their faces, even if he forgot their names, wheeled around and never looked back. When he reached the hotel where he had been staying he went inside to his room, gathered up all of his belongings, packed everything and his saddle bags, except for a clean pair of jeans and a clean shirt, which he rolled up and his bedroll. Then he went downstairs to the desk clerk and signed a voucher that he would pay for his stay there. He said goodbye and walked out the door, stepped back into the saddle and headed for the train depot and El Paso. It had taken the better part of two weeks to get from Austin Texas to El Paso, but the trip had been easy and he marveled at the changes in scenery in the state of Texas. It went from grassy fields in rivers, to desert and cactus and sand. There were oil wells everywhere you looked, dozens of them closely built together. He wondered if this would bring more outlaws to the state Of Texas, this stuff that they call black gold would be a thorn in the side of Texans. When he arrived at El Paso, he knew only to look for an office with a sign saying, Texas Ranger, so getting his horse from the cattle car. He rode slowly down the street looking on both sides. Finally he saw an office that said United States marshal, so he decided to stop and see if they could tell him where his office was. He pulled up in front, Dismounted and walked inside and a short, stocky young man stuck Out his hand and said," I'm a United States marshal. Trudeau, what can I do for your Ranger?Taking Marshall's hand, he said, "Sam Cooper, Texas Ranger, and I have no idea where my office is, I thought maybe you might know." Motioning for Sam to set down, Trudeau said "I sure do, but you're on the other side of town. Set down and rest a spell and then I'll show you where your office is, and if you're hungry, I'll show you the best place in town to eat." "Now that you mention it Marshall, I believe I could stand to eat something." Sam felt that Trudeau was a man to get to know. So he set down and for the next hour they spent time answering each other's questions, and finally Trudeau said "Let's go find your office and get you settled in, and then we'll go get a bite to eat. In the meantime, it won't take but just a minute to stop at the boarding house where you'll be staying and drop off your gear." "I can't keep calling you Marshall Trudeau, so what's your first name?" "I'll tell you but if you laugh, I will shoot you. My name is Millard Trudeau and I am from the state of Louisiana about half way between New Orleans and Baton Rouge. Where do you have a hale from? "I was born in a sharecropper shack just south of Little Rock, Arkansas, my parents moved to Texas, just west of Nacogdoches when I was six months old and we lived there until a band of outlaws murdered my family while I was picking up supplies in Nacogdoches. Then Ben Jonson Took me under his wing and got me into the rangers and now I'm here for better or worse. I am the Texas Ranger posted here and I hope that you and I can work together and not fight." Trudeau said. "I'll tell White, for the rest of the day, let's not talk business, let's just get acquainted and I'll show you around, so you'll know how to get around this town. There are 10 Mexicans to every white man, so I suggest that you learn to speak Spanish quickly." "I already speak a decent amount of Spanish, enough to communicate anyway. But I promise I will strive to learn more. Do you know of anybody that would take the time to teach me?" "Yes I do, and you'll meet her when we stop to have supper. She owns the little restaurant where the law man it, and we eat there because it is the best food in town barring none. Her name is Consuela Salazar and she is one nice lady." "How About the boarding house, well I have my own room, or will I have to share it with someone? "No, you'll have your own private room and you also have your own private entrance. You see, Mrs. Salazar owns the boarding house too, so you don't have to worry about anything. She will take extremely good care of you." Without any more questions to ask Sam concentrated on getting to know the business and the owners, because it seemed that everyone in town that he and Trudeau passed would waive their hand and say good evening in Spanish. Anyway, Sam was looking forward to a good meal, and a good night's rest. Trudeau took Sam to the Mexican side of town, and showed him his office. there was a tall young Mexican man inside the office cleaning up, when he seen Sam, He turned around and offered his hand in friendship and said," My name is Manuel and I have been hired to keep your office clean and help you in any way I can, Such as watching the office when you are gone, and making sure any prisoners you have are fed, picking up the mail for your office and delivering it. If there is anything else that you require all you have to do is ask." Seeing the kind of respect the Texas rangers badge received it made Sam feel like he had found a home once again. But this time, no one would rob it and burn it down or kill its occupants. "It's not a big office, but it will do! Sam said "The ranger who had this job before, he retired at the age of 52, he's got a little ranch, just east of here. I'd say probably 15 miles and he drops by from time to time, his name is Joe Sterling. He still feels like this office belongs to him, so don't let him bully you. When he comes into town, my advice to you is to tell him point blank that you are the one that wears the badge now. It won't hurt to listen to his advice, but let him know that his advice is not carved in stone, you don't have to take it." Trudeau made this statement while pointing at a small little restaurant across the street and motioning for Sam to follow him. When they walked into the restaurant, the smell of the food took him back to east Texas and his mom is cooking. At once he started getting the feeling of being home, and it felt good. He and Trudeau had no sooner than set down. When a middle-aged lady with long black hair and a big smile walked up to the table carrying a No sooner than set down. When a middle-aged lady with long black hair and a big smile walked up to the table carrying a pot of coffee and 2 cups. it was as if she knew what you wanted to eat by just looking at you .Sam looked at the lady and said , "I'm sorry ma'am, I don't speak a lot of Spanish , so I'll have to order in English , I hope you don't mind ," speaking in perfect English . She answered Sam , saying , "Don't worry about it cowboy , I'll have you speaking Spanish with the best of them before you can grow whiskers" then She turned around , went back to the kitchen and interests a couple of minutes she came out carrying two platters of food , one for Trudeau and one for him. She said it down in front of them, along with a bowl of salsa and a stack of tortillas, she then looked at Sam, winked and said, "Eat up, There's more where that came from." As the two men sat and ate, Trudeau was also pointing out businesses that lined the street stating his opinion of which businesses were good, and which were rip-offs. It seemed that he knew everyone and every business, personally or at least that's what he wanted you to think. Sam had taken a liking very quickly to this man, he had the same personality and friendliness of his oldest brother, and he liked that. When they had finished eating they sat for a while drinking coffee and talking about nothing in particular, just getting to know each other .Trudeau put down an empty cup and said, "Come on ranger and I'll show you where your horse will be kept and introduce you to the man who will take care of him for you, and then I will show you to the boarding house and I'll see you sometime tomorrow."Not knowing really what to do Sam walked up to the front door of the boarding house and knocked, a young lady answered the door and she asked, "Are you ranger cooper?" "Yes, ma'am, I guess I'm guilty." my Mother sent word that you would be here, I am to show you your room and see if there is anything else that you require. I am also to tell you that you will eat breakfast here and supper, lunch, you must eat at the restaurant. Enrique will take care of your horse for you each night, he is my brother and he runs the livery stable at the end of the street. He will feed, water, and rob down your animal each and every night and he will feed him in the mornings, then he will saddle your horse and bring it to the front of your office and tie him to the hitching post, and less it is raining, then the horse will stay in the stables. If you agree to all of this it will cost you $3 per week, and it will be charged to the Texas Rangers." Sam had stayed in a lot of hotels, but never a boarding house, there was a door in his room that he could come and go through without bothering anyone else, and what made it so nice was no one would know what time he came in or what time he left. He could also tell that this boarding house, except for around meal time was extremely quiet so it should be easy to get a good night's rest. That was something that Sam was going to find out immediately. He was tired and he felt like he could sleep for a week. He knew that was not a possibility, But it was a good idea anyway. After being shown his room, the young lady brought in a picture of water, a towel, a large bowl, and a bar of soap. Then she pointed out the door at a little outhouse that set at the back of the property. the young girl smiled at him and said , "There are no rules for that little building , you may use it whenever you have to." she then turned and left the room , but Sam would have sworn that she was flirting with him , maybe it was his imagination , but it sure made him feel good . It had been pointed out that he could lock both doors from the inside. there was no key , but there was a slight bolt on the inside of both doors , and to the door going outside there was a key hanging beside the door that locked it from the outside , sums up to himself , "This is nice , but it's almost like being in a jail . All of these locks could make a man awful nervous." Taking off his boots, his jeans, and his shirt, leaving nothing but his longjohns on, he started to lay down. Then he realized that he still had his hat and neckerchief on. So he mumbled to himself, "You better straighten up boy, or you'll have people thinking you're from the poor side of town, and ignorant as hell." Sam Stressed out on the bed and compared it to sleeping on the ground in a bedroom, it was like lying down on a cloud. He would later find out that it was a handmade shuck mattress, he didn't care, and it was comfortable. The next morning he was awakened by a gentle knocking on his door and a voice so sweet saying, "Breakfast will be served in 30 minutes." Sam sat up very quickly and replied, "Yes ma'am, I will be right there. Thank you." He had to admit he was kind of hungry, and he wondered what this lady would serve for breakfast, would it be Mexican style breakfast. Or would it be American style? Like ham and eggs, bacon and eggs, steak and eggs, pancakes and eggs? Finally, Sam decided to stop guessing and just get out there in the dining room and find out what was for breakfast, he thought to himself, "Whatever it is, I hope there's a lot of it." Not knowing what to expect when he walked into the dining room, Sam just to there for a moment, the young lady seen him and walked over to a seat and pulled it out and said "As long as you stay in our boarding house, this will be your seat always" Without asking any more questions Sam sat down and watched as the food was put on the table. There was a platter of fried eggs, a platter that contained bacon, sausage, and ham. There was also a large bowl of fried potatoes, another large bowl full of gravy, and there were two platters stopped completely with biscuits. There was coffee, sweet milk, and buttermilk and then right in the middle of the table was a medium-sized bowl of salsa. Sam thought to himself "If I leave this table still hungry, that's my fault!" After he had eaten his fill Sam said, "Ma'am, that is the best meal that I have ever had for breakfast, I am so full I may have to walk a couple of miles before I can get on my Horse, I wouldn't want to hurt him." with a big smile, she looked at Sam and said, "Thank you, I am glad you enjoyed it, will you be here for supper? It will be served at 7:00 sharp." "Yes, ma'am, the only thing that will keep me from being here for supper, is if someone decides to rob the bank." "If somebody does rob the bank it would do this town good" "What Do you mean, ma'am?" " That banker will sell someone land and then the first chance he gets , he will foreclose on it and resell it for the same price that he sold it for to start with . There are people in this town that have lived and worked land for 15 years made every payment, then when the sickness hit, they got one or two payments behind and the bank would not work with them, they evicted them without giving them a chance to make up the missed payments. There are a lot of people in this town who would like to see that banker strung up, because they believed that he has stolen from a lot of people." "Did He steal from you, Ms. Salazar?" "He tried, but I had money put back. He wanted to take my boarding house , my Livery stable , and my restaurant and I was not even one payment behind , I was two weeks late , but I was not behind!" Right away, Sam knew he had to talk to Trudeau about This banker and get his thoughts on the man. As much as Trudeau liked Mrs. Salazar, Same could not understand why he hadn't lowered the boom on this banker. That was something seemed and Trudeau would have a lengthy conversation about. Thanking Ms. Salazar once again for a delicious breakfast. Sam got up from the table and said, "I have a few things I have to check into today, so I best be getting on my way, or else with all this food in my stomach, I might just have to lay down and take a nap." Without saying anything else Sam grabbed his hat and stepped out on the porch before he put it on. He was taught that it was employed to wear a hat inside of a house, a church, or a restaurant. He had been taught that and he was not going to go against that teaching now or ever. He decided he was going to walk all the way to Trudeau's office, just because he felt he needed the exercise, and besides he needed to meet as many people as he possibly could. The people needed to know that he was here to protect them and to help them anyway that he could , so if it meant spending a little time talking to the people on the sidewalks or the owners of the businesses ,Then so be it . This was his town, and he needed to learn to love, not just part of it, but all of it. As Trudeau had said this town was made up of 90% Mexican, 10% Caucasian. Besides being raised in east Texas in his youth he was introduced to the influences of that Cherokee Indian, The French, and the African-American. Then you had people that moved out from Boston who were mainly Irish. From New York were mainly Italian.

Same had been raised to learn something from every person he met, to take something with him while at the same time leaving something behind, a part of himself. Making sure that everyone he met got a good look at his badge and had the opportunity to speak to him, and if they did he took the time to talk to them as best he could in Spanish. He needed these people to understand that he was their friend and he would treat everyone the same, no matter what their nationality. It took the better part of three hours for Sam to make it to Trudeau's office, Sam walked directly to the coffee pot and poured him a cup of coffee. Then he went over to the chair that sat in front of Trudeau's desk, sat down and said, "Tell me about this banker that keeps foreclosing on people, and getting robbed!" "Well, good morning to you too!" and Trudeau said with a smile, "I see you've been talking to some of the locals." "Yes I have, and Trudeau I'm not really liking the stories that I'm hearing, especially from Mrs. Salazar. Why haven't you checked into this banker?" "I have Sam, I know the man is crooked and I know the man has had his own bank robbed. I know this man has had people killed. I just can't prove it". Trudeau said this as he clenched his fists and shook it slightly while gritting his teeth. Sam was quite sure that Trudeau was an honest man and that he wasn't a small man. He just didn't have the resources that he needed, such as getting someone inside the bank, a teller, or a bookkeeper, to keep him informed of things that's going on inside the bank. Maybe he could do something about that. "How many people would you say this banker has foreclosed on? And of the people he has foreclosed on, how many has turned up dead or missing, or reportedly has packed up and left?" Sam was looking at Trudeau, right in the eye when he asked these questions. "There have been quite a few Sam, but if I can't find them or their bodies there is nothing I can do about it. I have to have some kind of proof before I can make any kind of a move at all. And believe me that banker needs to be put completely out of business, Maybe we can work together and accomplish this." "Maybe so," Sam said as he leaned back in his chair. Trudeau looked at Sam and asked, "How did you get here? I didn't hear no horse right up!" "I walked" Sam answered,

"And I had a lot of good conversations with people who have concerns about the businesses in this town. I got the impression that a lot of these businesses are not very trustworthy and are exploiting the Mexican population, but if somebody tried to do something about it, they suddenly either disappear or get beat up." "That's about the sides of it Sam, But if the people want to talk to you and tell you what happened, there is not a whole lot that you can do." "I don't believe that Trudeau, I believe in fighting fire with fire, and I think we need to light a fire! Who do you consider to be the most corrupt businessmen in this town?" "That's easy Sam, there are two, the banker and the man who owns the saloon." Sam rubbed his chin, then scratched his head, then finally said, "What say me and you go over to the saloon and have a beer?" "What have you got on your mind, Sam?" Trudeau asked with a puzzled look on his face. With a chuckle, Sam said, "If Think I'm about to build me a fire, ok, with you?" Getting up from his chair Trudeau, smiled and said, "Lead the way, my good man, lead the way." They were only about a block away from the saloon, so instead of riding their horses they walked. Sam noticed that Trudeau's war has gone a little higher than most law men that told Sam he was not very fast with his side arm, but then again you can never tell until you see a man use it. While walking, I guess Trudeau felt he had to make a confession because he started talking, "I usually carry a shotgun with me everywhere I go, but I kind of thought this visit at least ought to look friendly." Then he chuckled and mumbled, "I can already taste that beer, can't you?" The two men walked into the saloon. Giving the appearance that they were just there to have a beer and sit and talk. All the time both men were watching the games that were going on, and write-off Sam noticed, there were at least six man standing in posted positions all around the gaming tables .Trudeau looked across the room and said, "Oh, Get ready, here comes the man that owns this place." The owner walked up to the table with a smile on his face that just seemed to make Sam skin crawl. He started out speaking to Trudeau, "I see you finally decided to visit my establishment and if see you brother friend." Although Sam had not been spoken to, he spoke up. "Names Sam cooper and I've been told the old games are cooked and I'm here to give you notice that I will be checking from time to time , and if I find anything wrong , I will close you down and running out of town ." "Just who the hell do you think you are?" He said, "Like I said, my name is Sam cooper and I'm a Texas Ranger, and I've been sent here to help martial Trudeau clean up this town at to get rid of the undesirables." The owner of the saloon turned around and left a table where Sam and Trudeau were seated. When he was out of earshot Trudeau looked at Sam And said, "Start a fire my ass, you just started a forest fire! You so much as told him that you were coming after him." "Yes sir, I do believe that's the way he took it. You see the way I look at things is very simple, if he wasn't doing anything wrong, then it wouldn't bother him half as much. So by his actions he has pretty much admitted that his games are cooked, now all if have to do is prove it. I am pretty sure that I can find somebody that I can trust, who will come in here and play and keep his eyes open and his mouth shut. Have you ever seen the owner of the saloon and the banker spend any amount of time together?" "As a matter of fact I have," Trudeau said. " If I'm not badly mistaken they either meet at the bank on Monday or here at the saloon Monday evening , I never dawned on me before , but it's a pretty regular thing ." "Are the guards inside this place always with him?" "As a matter of fact, yes, but they also escort every morning the money that displays made the night before to the bank. I have been there when they came in and they always go straight back to the banks owners private office. I must be getting too relaxed in my job, because none of this stuff, I ever really paid attention to. But you are right, I think it's just found some rotten sauerkraut!" The two men finished their beer and politely got up and walked out. "What do we do now Sam? What is your plan?" "Right now I am going to the bank and notify the bank owner that I am having a state auditor to come in and start an investigation into the last robbery that occurred in this bank. And also I am instructing the auditor to take statements from all witnesses and bank customers who lost money." With a smile and a wink Sam is strolled off in the direction of the bank, Trudeau just laugh and said to himself, "I like that Feller". Taking his time and stopping to talk to people, and visiting a few of the businesses along the way. Sam kept an eye out for any of the men who worked for the saloon owner to see if they made a beeline for the bank. He had no doubts that these two people were as Crooked As a barrel of fish hooks, and he intended to prove it. Sam walked into the bank and asked to see the owner, the teller turned around, walked over to the office door and knocked then went in, and a few seconds later came out and motioned for Sam to come on behind the counter. Holding the door open he motioned for Sam to go inside the office. Sitting behind a big mahogany desk was a very muscular, dark-haired man who, without much success pretended to be a friendly man. "What can I do for you ranger?" He asked while holding out his hand." I was thinking about opening up a bank account but I'm not too sure about your bank. After all it has been robbed a total of six times in the past three years. Do youcarry insurance that will replace the money of your customers when a robbery occurs? If you don't, if am going to call in the state bank examiner and the state auditor and we are going to find out why." Sam had never sat down and after his statement the bank owner's mouth was open and he had stunned look on his face, so, some shook his hand, then turn around without saying anything else. Deciding that he had stirred up as much trouble as he possibly could, some headed back up to the marshal's office, Halfway expecting somebody to shoot at him, but nothing happened. When he entered the marshal's office, Trudeau was sitting behind his desk and with a big smile he asked, "Well, did you tell him you were calling in the army, or just a platoon of rangers." "No, I just told him I was sending for the state bank examiner and the state bank auditor and find out why he didn't carry insurance to cover his customer's money and if left it at that." Sam answered. "I would bet money that within the next 2 hours, you will start seeing a lot of activity between the saloon and the bank. They have got to in some way cover up whatever they have been doing. I kept out of this Marshall and purpose, I want you to play a role, I want you to go back to both of these men and apologize for my actions.

Make them think that you are looking out for them. Meanwhile, I am pretty sure that someone will take a shot at me. Do you have anybody in mind that you trust absolutely?" "I sure do." Trudeau answered. "Well, would you do me a favor and get a hold of this person and tell him or her that you need them to watch my back?" Sam told Trudeau that he was going back to his office, and maybe go by the restaurant and get some lunch. Anyway, he would be one place or the other. have the man very quietly introduced himself to me ,So I won't think he's the person Who was sent to shoot me in the back . then Sam left the marshal's office slowly walking back toward the Mexican side of town .But this time he quickened his pace not because he was anticipating a bullet in the back, but simply because he was hungry .Arriving at the restaurant, Sam glanced at his pocket watch and it was 1:30 in the afternoon and the restaurant only had four or five customers. Sam got him a table in the corner and looked at the menu board, quickly deciding that he wanted to have the lunch special. Miss Salazar had seen him come in and had given him enough time to set down before she came to the table. He looked at her and smiled, but when he started to talk, she cut him off by saying, "We have heard about what you did in the saloon, are you trying to commit suicide, you know these men will try to kill you." Sam looked at her and smiled and said very softly, "Then Miss Salazar I will wake west that I do not die with an empty stomach, May I have the lunch special and a large glass of buttermilk?" "Are you sure that you have not been hit in the head or something that has rattled your brain? If these people come after you, they will not care who else gets shot." "Don't worry Miss Salazar, until this thing is settled I won't be staying at the boarding house. I will not put you and your family and danger, so I suggest that you, your son, and your daughter, stay as far away from me as you can possibly get." "But sir, if we do that, where would you eat, where would you sleep? No, I will not let you isolate yourself to protect us. You are doing your job and if we are not willing to stand up beside you, then we don't deserve you as our protector. So you will sleep in your room, you will eat at the boarding house and here. That is all I have to say about the matter!" Sam thought to himself, "what a woman". After he had his lunch Sam decided to go into his office and see if any male had come in. He hadn't been given any orders except to report to this post, and take over. There had to be a reason why that he had been sent so far from Austin, he just couldn't figure out what it was. But nevertheless he was here and he had a job to do and he was going to do it. when he arrived at his office, he found Manuel cleaning out the cells in the back, He had already taken the mattresses out back and beat them to remove the dust, Then he had taken them back inside put them on the bunks And put a folded up blanket along with a pillow on each mattress. He had swept and mopped the floor, took a broom and knock down all of the cobwebs and was now cleaning the main office. Seeing Sam he asked, if you was doing the job the way he was supposed to, Sam patted him on the shoulder and told him he was doing a fine job and that he had no complaints whatsoever. Manuel Then pointed to Sam's desk, and there was a stack of mail that had not been opened, Saw Sam set down and proceeded to open and read every letter and every package. He found two large envelopes of wanted posters, there was a letter from ben Johnson, and there was another letter from the main office at ranger's headquarters. Sam decided he would save that one till last. He pulled out all of the wanted posters and handed them to Manuel and he proceeded to put them on the bulletin board so that anyone who came into the office could see them .Sam asked Manuel "Are you going to be around the office the rest of the day?" "Yes sir, I will be here till 6 o'clock unless you want me to stay longer?" "No, by then I will be back at the boarding house, and then maybe I might go to the saloon and get a beer." "If I need you. You will be one of two places?" Sam Nodded his head unanswered. "Yes, but if you don't see me, find Marshall Trudeau, he will know where if am at". In the meantime, Trudeau had gone over to the saloon and apologized to the owner for Sam's actions and Assured him that he would keep close tabs on Sam. then he went to the bank on done the same thing, all the time, hoping that these two despicable man make a mistake. Even noticed Sam walking down the boardwalk, so he waved at him and cross the street to meet. "Just where do you think you're going ranger?" "I thought I go to the saloon and get a beer." Sam Replied. "There is a small cantina right on down the street that has exceptionally cold beer, that's where I'm going, how about joining me?" Seeing that Trudeau was trying to keep him out of the saloon for some reason. Sam said in a normal tone of voice. "Sure Why not, it's just another place where I can get to know the people." The two men started walking down the boardwalk, and Trudeau was pointing out each and every business and telling him about the owners of each business. He told how long each one had been in El Paso and if they were born there or moved there. As soon as they were out of sight of the saloon. Trudeau said, "Are you trying to get killed? They are lying in wait for you, so watch your step Sam!"

CHAPTER 2

The little cantina was a real nice place. The waitresses were friendly and quite pretty, the beer was cold, the tequila strong, and the music was loud. Trudeau and Sam Sat at a corner table with their backs to the wall and their eyes on the room .Trudeau looked at Sam and quietly spoke "The trusted friend that you asked me about, He is watching your back, and he said to tell you that he would get in touch with you tomorrow at noon at miss Sanchez's restaurant." "Thanks Trudeau, I owe you one." "Sam, just to be on the safe side tonight, why don't you spend the night at my office. There is a cot in the little room between the main office and the jail. The door can be barred from the inside, and the windows have bars on them, so as long as you don't stand in front of a window no one will be able to get to you. The building is An Adobe building, so it won't burn. I really think it will be the smart thing to do Sam". Working on his second beer and second shot of tequila, Sam, nodded his head Yes, Trudeau leaned back in his Chair and let out a big sigh of relief. For the first time since he had known Sam he had talked him into doing something that would be best for him. "If I stay at your office, where are you going to stay?" "I've got a room at the hotel that I used when I don't have any prisoners, and I don't have any prisoners, so the place is all yours." "You do realize that you have to wake up in the morning, if you're used to get an early start, because it's been a long time since I have been able to lay down and sleep without being on edge. I agree with you Trudeau, I think I really do need some quiet time with no distractions to get what I am going to do straight in my mind. I have baited the hook now i need to find out if the fish are going to bite." This reminded Sam of the time that his father and his two brothers and him took off to the Arkansas

River to set out some trot lines and see if they could get a good mess of fish, so they could have a fish fry at the little country church they attended about halfway between their home and Nacogdoches. they spent all night and half of the next day catching catfish and putting them in pens to keep them alive Until they were ready to clean them all at the same time. They ended up catching almost 130 catfish Off of four trot lines. Sam remembered just how sick he got of cleaning catfish, but they got them cleaned and got them to the church and the Ladies cooked 130 pounds catfish, hush puppies and coleslaw, and they must have made 20 gallon of sweet iced tea. He remember that he ate so much catfish that day that he has never wanted catfish since. Trudeau said to Sam, "You know it's awfully funny to remember things like that, usually things like that pop up in your mind when you are nervous or on edge. I used to have things come to me like that , but then my wife left me , took my only child and went back east , Where she was from , and I haven't had a thought like that since she left ." "This is going to sound crazy to you, Trudeau's, but I am a firm believer in god, reincarnation, ghosts, and angels. I have seen too many things that I cannot explain, from curses been put on people, to curses being taken off of people. I have been to places that I know I have never been before, but yet I could draw you a detailed map of the entire town and name every store and in its proper location. I have met people that there is no way that I have ever met them before, but yet I know everything there is to know about them. There are times when I know what is going to happen, and no matter how hard I try I can't change .I will tell you something now Trudeau that is going to blow your mind. I'm going to die young, and I will die a very violent deaths and you Trudeau will play a big part in bringing my killer to justice. It will not be you that brings him in, but someone that you become extremely fond of and you also become part of his life as I have become part of yours. It will be you, Trudeau, that will find my body and it will be you who bear is it. I am going to apply to the United States Marshal's office for a job, and I will be accepted, I have seen this in a dream. the badge that I wear when I joined you as a martial will become a very special and powerful badge, not to be borne by you, but to be won by a very special an honest man who does not really want to wear it , but does under strenuous circumstances. It will bring him fame and he will find the love of a very special woman. Mark my words, Trudeau all of this will come to pass and not too far in the future." Trudeau just sat and looked at Sam, and then he said, "Ranger don't believe the things you said. Cannot handle your tequila because it makes you see things that are not there, and lets you say things that can't happen. I guess we better call it a night and get you to bed so you can sober up." "Mark my words Millard, what I have told you will happen, and only after my death will you believe, because you will see it with your own eyes and you will feel with your heart". Without saying anything else, Sam got up from the table, and walked out the door. Trudeau finished his beer and went out the door to try to catch up with him, but he was nowhere in sight, it was as if he had vanished! So just to check he walked up to the marshal's office and went inside, but Sam cooper was not there. Knowing best Sam had not ridden a horse, there was no way that he could have vanished that quickly and since he did not believe in the supernatural, he was afraid that something had happened to cooper. Maybe he needed to go to bed and get some rest, also. Sam had taking his time walking home to the boarding house, he wasn't worried anymore. He knew the way things were going to end, so all he could do was solve the problems that he can now, and let the future take care of itself. He entered the boarding house through the side door that went into his room, and being as quiet as he possibly could. he and rest and laid down on that wonderfully soft shuck mattress And he wondered if he had disturbed Trudeau by telling him the way things were going to be , and telling him of things that he could not believe now , but within time's to come. Lay his head back on his pillow, He thanked god for a good day and for his life, and with peace in his heart, he went to sleep, knowing in his heart that he had a certain amount of days left he intended to solve as many problems as he possibly could, And tomorrow he would write a letter to the united states marshals main office, introduced himself and apply to become a united states

Marshal, and request to be position in central Texas, hopefully in El Paso. When the sun came up that next morning, it found Sam already dressed and waiting to be told that breakfast was on the table. He had gotten very fond of Miss Salazar and her children, the whole family was a hard-working, god fearing group of people, who believed in saying and doing the right thing. They were the kind of people that just being around them made you feel at ease. As he sat on the edge of his bad a gentle mac come on his door and a voice said, "Wake up, Sam breakfast will be on the table in 30 minutes." "Yes, ma'am, and thank you." was Sam's reply. There was so much put on the table for breakfast that no one minded that it was the same every morning. The same food was on the table, but you could have a different breakfast every morning. The only thing that you could request that wasn't on the table was scrambled eggs, instead of fried. Sam was a firm believer that breakfast with the most important meal of the day, and he made sure every morning that he had a good breakfast. Miss Salazar looked at Sam, smiled and asked," Did you have a good time last night at the Cantina?" "I don't know, I don't remember much about last night, except that the beer was cold, the tequila was strong, and the music was loud. That's when everything goes fuzzy, I really don't remember coming home last night. If I woke you up, or disturbed you in any way I apologize."! "The only reason why I heard you last night is because I was up in the kitchen doing my books and getting my deposit ready to go in the bank." "Is there another bank anywhere near hear that you can put your money in?" Sam asked. "Yes , there is , it's quite a bit further away than the one I'm using now , I have seriously been considering changing banks . Maybe I should!". "Before you open up your restaurant this morning, why don't you have your son hook up a buggy for you and take a trip down to the other bank and ask them some questions. Make sure that you ask them if they carry insurance that covers your money in your account if they are rubbed." Getting up from the table Sam thanked Miss Salazar for a lovely meal, then told her that he would be at the restaurant around lunch time. He then said goodbye to everyone else and walked out the door. He put his hat on then sat down in a chair that was on the porch and proceeded to roll him a cigarette. He leaned back in the chair and study the people who wear on the street and watched to see what time the businesses open their doors. One of the ways that you can tell that something was not right, is if a business does not open at the same time every day .A lot of robberies have been averted by an alert law man, Noticing that a business that has a reputation for being punctual does not open at its normal time, when it doesn't it needs to be investigated very quietly. Sam sat there for a little while longer, just watching the people and smoking his cigarette. Finally he decided it was time for him to put in an appearance at the office, and at least act like he was earning his money. So getting up lazily he started in the direction of the ranger station. Taking his time and speaking to everyone he met, Sam was beginning to like this town. When he stepped into the office Manuel was as nervous as he could be, he grabbed a wanted poster off of the board and handed it to Sam and said, " I seen this man in the saloon last night talking to the man who owns it, and with that banker from just down the street . They were sitting in the back, all three of them at a table and they were speaking very quietly. I just thought you might want to know Ranger" "Are you absolutely sure this is the man you saw last night?" "Yes sir, I had just put up the poster and you can't mistake the scar he has over his left eye. I understand that the law man, put it there"! "Manuel, can you get the Marshall's office and asked Trudeau to meet me in the saloon. If he wants to know why, tell him. Also tell him to bring his shotgun, and to act like he is just making his rounds early in the morning. I'll give you 15 minutes! That should be enough time for you to get to Trudeau and Trudeau to get to the saloon, now scoot."!! You would have thought somebody had tied a string of fire crackers to him because he lit out down the street at a dead run, so Sam figured he'd better start walking that way because Manuel would be at Trudeau's office before Sam got halfway to the saloon. So stepping out at a good pace. Sam stayed on the side of the street that the saloon was on. As he was walking down the street he noticed a tall younger gentleman following him so he stepped in between two buildings and stopped when the young man got to where Sam had turned in between the two buildings, he reached out and grabbed him by the shirt collar and pulled him in between the two buildings. The young threw up his hands and said "whoa!" "Whoa hell, what are you doing follow me?" Looking at Sam through cold dark eyes. The stranger smiled. "Trudeau sent me, said I needed to watch your back for a while"

Sam looked at the feller, and dropped his head. Let out a groan and said, "Damn, I forgot all about me being supposed to meet you at Miss Sanchez's at lunch, so I would know who you are, my apologies Sir. My name is Sam Cooper, what's yours?"

My name is Luis Gonzales, and I work for the Marshall, by keeping my ears and eyes open and my mouth shut."!

Do you ever go into the saloon? Sam asked, the young man needed his head eyes. "I want you to wait a couple of minutes after I go in. Then you come in and get in a position where you can cover my back. I sent word for the Marshall to meet me there, so be looking for him, and if you can catch him before he comes inside tell him what you're doing, and that I asked you to do it.

Luis didn't say anything, he just turned and started walking toward the saloon and then kind of wandered out into the middle of the street as if he had already had one's too many .

As Sam approached the saloon he noticed that Luis had already run into the Marshall. They were standing in the middle of the street and the Marshall was reading him the riot act over being drunk this early morning. Luis was telling the Marshall that his girlfriend had just broke up with him, and he would go home and sleep it off, but he wanted to get one more drink, so the Marshall agreed to let him have one more beer, and the two men started walking toward the saloon. Seeing this Sam went ahead and entered the saloon walked up to the bar and ordered a beer after all it was already quite warm outside.

Looking around the room it didn't take long for Sam to spot the guy whose face was on the wanted poster. He was standing at the bar drinking a beer and talking to the saloon owner. Sam finished his beer was just about to call the man's name. When the Marshall and Luis walked through the door and walked straight to the bar right next to the man he had come after. Luis ordered a beer and the Marshall reached in his left vest pocket and with his left hand laid some change on the bar, and with his right hand pulled his 45 and put the muzzle into the many ribs and told him not to move. Sam stepped away from the bar and noticed a feller sitting at a table directly behind the Marshall go for his gun, he had just managed to clear leather when Sam fired. The man lunged backwards into another table and fell to the floor.

Trudeau looked at Sam, nodded his head. "Thanks for watching my back, would you mind helping me get this fellow to the jail?" "No sir, not at all"

"Joseph lane, you are under arrest for bank robbery and murdered, now walk" Trudeau said as he headed the man toward the front door. Sam asked the Marshall to hold up just a minute, and he walked up to the saloon owner and whispered something in his ears, then took a step back, smiled and said to Trudeau, "okay, Marshall, now we can go."!

As the two men escorted lane to the Marshall's office, Sam kept a close eye to the saloon door and the windows of the second floor, he didn't really expect any trouble because this arrest had happened so quickly, it kind of left the saloon owner a little dazed.

After a prisoner had been locked away Trudeau turned to Sam and ask, "Okay, what did you say to baker?" "I told him to stick around. I'd be back to see him later about harboring a fugitive." Sam replied.

"What are you trying to do? Force him into making a move," with a very stern look and stone face, Sam said, "yes sir, that's exactly what I'm trying to get him to do. I want him and this banker to understand that I am looking at them through a magnifying glass, I want them to understand that I know their dirty and I am going to prove it."!

Well, I just hope you know what you're doing. These people will not come at you head on, but they will shoot you in the back from ambush, you can rest assured of that"

"By the way Trudeau, why did you step in between me and lane?" "You said you wanted to be a Marshall, well we are instructed to handle things a little different than the rangers. We are instructed to bring a prisoner in if at all possible, to stand trial. I knew that you were going to call this man out and give him only two choices draw, or back down. I just thought that I would save us both a lot of paperwork, besides the judge hasn't earned his pay for this month yet."

"Okay then, you've got lane, and I've got things to do. I'm going to be at Mrs. Salazar's in about 45minutes, if you can why don't you join me for lunch, I always did hate to eat alone."

"I just may do that, but don't hold me to it, Trudeau said. I've got to call in my part-time deputy, he only works when I have prisoners. Me meeting you for lunch. Depends on how fast I can find him."

Sam got up, threw up his hand in a gesture of goodbye and stepped out onto the boardwalk. Pausing to roll himself a cigarette and light it, all the time studying the buildings around the saloon and especially the second floor windows, but he seen nothing suspicious. He then turned and headed for Miss Salazar's and a tasty lunch.

It seemed that everyone in El Paso had something to say to Sam, because it took him over an hour to get Ms. Salazar's, and how he done it Sam couldn't figure out, but Trudeau was already there.

He looked up at Sam and ask, "Just where in the hell have you been? I was beginning to worry about you."!

It seemed that everyone on the street has some kind of a question to ask me, or some kind of a problem that they wanted me to help them solve. One fella said that someone was stealing his horses, riding them, and then bringing them back. I told him that in my way of thinking. It was kids, and if he would just be patient he would catch them."

Trudeau said to Sam "I have to take a ride this afternoon, I was wondering if you would like to accompany me? It's about time you got to know some of the people around here. Sam said. "Sure"

There are some mighty fine people around here. And the ranch that I'm going to take you to are some of the really upstanding people. The Arnett's are hard-working ranchers and they do a lot for the people in the community. As long as I have been there, they have never asked me for anything except if I would come out to the ranch and have Sunday dinner with them. I kind of figure that they should get to know you, and that you should absolutely get to know them"

Is there anything special going on? Or is this one of those missions where you just remind the people that you know they're still out there! And if they need anything please don't hesitate to ask."

"Yeah, that's more or less what this trip to about, but you'll understand why I make it when you meet the Arnett's. You'll never meet a more friendly family, or people who respect the law any more than they do."

"Well, what do you say Marshall, less eat our lunch, let it settle for little while , by the way , how long do you think this trip is going to take us? Do you think we'll back before sundown?" "I'd say probably 3 to 4 hours out there and back should cover it. It's 15 minutes till one now, so you should be back no later than five."

"You seem to think quite a lot of these people, how long have you known them?" "Ever since I've been here in El Paso," Trudeau said

As the two men sat there talking and drinking coffee, Mrs. Salazar walked over to the table and asked if there was anything else that they would like to have? Trudeau asked her, "Ms. Salazar, do you know the Arnett's that live out east of here?"

"Yes, I do Marshall, they were here when I got here, and incidentally they were the ones that made it possible for me to keep my boarding house and my little restaurant when that crocked banker tried to take it."

"What did the Arnett's do?" Sam asked.

"It was right after a robbery and all of my money was gone, there was no money left in the bank, I had some money here at the house, but if I used it I wouldn't have anything to operate on. The Arnett's heard of my predicament and they paid my loan off at the bank, which it was only a couple of hundred dollars, and told me to pay them back when I could. I worked hard, stayed open late, scrimped and saved. It took a while, but I got them paid back. I have admired them and counted them as friends.... Every sense, I do remember that banker got awfully mad at the Arnett's I remember him telling Mr. Arnett that it would be a good idea if he would mind his own business from now. But of course Mr. Arnett didn't pay any attention to him, as a matter of fact, Mr. Arnett called him a thief, and also told him that he was going to do everything in his to put him out of business, even if it meant opening his own bank."

"Did Mr. Arnett and this banker feller have any more dealings or any more run-ins?" Sam asked.

No one knows for sure if it was the banker or someone else, but on his way back to the ranch, about three months later, someone took a shot at him, but they missed, but Mr. Arnett seem to know who was behind it, but he used to say, he just couldn't prove it."

Sam looked over at Trudeau and said "yes sir, Marshall I would love to accompany you out to the Arnett's ranch. I hope you don't mind if I ask Mr. Arnett a few questions concerning the banker."

Trudeau got that big friendly smile on his face, "I really don't see that it would hurt, besides that was before I got here and the funny thing is Mr. Arnett has never mentioned that episode to me, I wonder what?"

After thanking Ms. Salazar for the information and complementing her on her cooking. The two men left the restaurant and headed for the livery stable to get their horses. While they were saddling their horses neither man said anything, it was as if they were both thinking the same thing. On their way out of town Sam stopped by his office and picked up a Winchester. Trudeau did the same, but he also picked up a double barreled shotgun.

Sam asked Trudeau, "You expecting a war?" never go anywhere without it, this old shotgun has stopped a lot of trouble before it ever stated."

With Trudeau leading the way, the two men headed east out of town. As they rode past the saloon, Sam noticed, all four of the so-called guards were standing outside the saloon, he also noticed the saloon owner coming out of the bank. Sam thought to himself, "Maybe they're planning another bank robbery, might be worth checking into."

When they had gotten out of town far enough, Trudeau slowed his horses to a walk. He then looked over at Sam and ask, "Did you get the same feeling that I did, as we was leaving town?"

"You mean the feeling that you get on the back of your neck when you're being watched? If that's what you're talking about Trudeau, then yes, I've felt the same chill in my back."!

Sam was riding and keeping an eye all the way around them, especially on the high spots and the gully's. Thank God, there was not a whole lot of trees in this section of Texas. Trudeau noticed that Sam seemed nervous, so he asked, "Do you really think they would try bushwhack two lawman at one time?"

Yes, I do, I think these men are ruthless enough that they think they can get by with anything, after all, I'm quite sure that the man who runs the saloon and the man that owns the bank and those four men who are supposed ti be guards for the saloon, are mixed up in these robberies all the way up to their chin."

"We're right in the middle of a lot of flat ground, and for once I'm glad of it. I don't think they can get close enough to us to get off a good clean shot, but less not tempt fate, put the spurs to your horse and less get on out to the Arnett's."! Trudeau said.

Spurring their horses into a good steady gallop, the two men left the trail and headed out in a straight line to the Arnett's ranch. It took the better part of an hour before they seen the ranch house.

Sam thought to himself, "Well, we made it this far, if we watch our step and take a different route back to town, we just might throw a cold bucket of water on their parade and not shed any blood doing it."

When they rode up to the ranch house, they were met by a man with a weather beaten face, and the lady that you could tell in her younger days was a beauty, because she still carried herself that way.

Trudeau spoke first, "Howdy Mr. Arnett, ma'am, I thought I'd bring this young feller out and introduce him to you, this is the new ranger in town, folks, I would like for you to meet Sam Cooper."

"Well, don't set up their on those horses like you're nailed to them, get down and come on in the house, I'm pretty sure that I've got a big pitcher of lemonade that should be just about ready to drank" Mrs. Arnett said with a big smile.

The next hour was spent answering questions from the Arnett's, and because they asked, Sam told them the story of how he became a Texas Ranger, he told them also about the murder of his entire family. There was still quite a few things that Sam left out. Then it was his turn to ask questions and when he asked questions about the banker, all Mr. Arnett would say was "he's a thief and a liar and I don't trust him as far as I can throw him."!!

There is a lot of people in El Paso, who share the same opinion of that banker as you do, it's none of my business Sir, but where do you do your banking? I surely hope that you do it with the other bank in town."

As a of fact, the only one who does any business with that bank is my daughter, and I can assure you that she puts no more money in that bank than she has to. Her biggest account is in the bank on the extreme eastern side of the city. From what Ms. Salazar says you don't care too much for the man that owns that bank either Ranger"

"No, Sir, I surely do not like that man, nor do I like or trust the man that runs the saloon. I personally believe that those two gentlemen are solely responsible for all of the robberies that has happened at the bank in the past three years. Any bank that has been robbed that many times would go out of business, but instead this bank seems to be getting stronger, to me. That means that there is something crocked going on, and I intend to find out what it is and who's behind it."

Trudeau spoke up and said, "I hate to put a damper on this party, but Sam if we're going to make it back to town before sunset. I think we best be getting on our way. We'll have to ride pretty hard as it stands, I'd say it's only a little more than an hour till the sun goes down."

Sam stood up, shook hands with Mr. Arnett, then he allowed Miss Arnett to give him a hug, which Sam thought was a very nice gesture on her part, after all, he hadn't been hugged by a lady in years.

While Trudeau was saying his goodbyes, Sam was already out the front door and sitting on his horse waiting. When Trudeau finally showed up. Sam looked over at him and ask, "Just exactly how far is it, as the crow flies back to town."? "I'd say seven or 8miles more or less." Trudeau answered.

Sam motioned for Trudeau to lead the way. Trudeau seemed to have learned this area very well in the time that he has been here, so Sam was quite content to follow behind. As long as he was behind Trudeau he could think, but if he got up beside Trudeau, he couldn't think because all Trudeau wanted to do was talk, and he would talk about anything and everything, and never take a hard breath.

The two men kept a steady pace all the way back to town but instead of coming in on the south side of town, Trudeau had circled around and they were coming in from the north side. The sun was just starting to set when they pulled up in front of Ms. Salazar. Sam looked at Trudeau and ask, "Are you going to join to me tonight, or do I have to eat alone again?

"Sam you're to have to get married if you want company every night while you're eating supper, just hanging around you. I have gained 15 or 20 pounds, and it's all in my stomach."

Ms. Salazar came out of the kitchen and walked directly to their table and said, "I heard about the way that you to left out of town, everyone seemed to think that you were after somebody, "No ma'am," Sam answered, "we just decided that our horses needed some exercise those horses and getting ourselves used to being back in the saddle, but as far as anything wrong… there isn't."

When she had gotten their order she turned and went back into the kitchen. Trudeau looked at Sam and said, "I don't know what think about you Ranger you are getting to the place where you can stretch the truth a long way, exercising the horses, I never heard such bull."

Well, I had to tell her something, I couldn't just up and tell her that we were looking into that banker and the saloon keeper, In my way of thinking that would've set her off and she would of went and give him a piece of her mind and maybe told him what we were planning to do, I just didn't want to take a chance on that."!

"Why do you think she would've done something like that Sam?" Trudeau asked, "I thought you liked her, and I sincerely thought you trusted her" "I do like her, and I do trust her, it's that Mexican temper that I don't trust. You know these Mexican women have got a temper and when they get mad, they're just apt to try to find the biggest man in the place and smacked him right dead across the mouth."

"I guess you're right Sam, but I still don't like not telling her the truth, but I guess your reasoning is sound enough. Aw hell, who am I kidding, you're right about the whole thing. She would probably be the first one to tell you, that is exactly what she would do."!

Ms. Salazar saved Sam from any more conversation because she showed up with their supper, and Sam thought to himself, "Thank God, maybe now we can talk about something else, or at least just eat our supper."

Other than saying how good supper was, there just wasn't much conversation at all. Both men were too busy eating. Ms. Salazar returned with a big pot of coffee and two cups, she asked if they would like to have dessert Sam simply said, "ma'am, if I eat another bite, I'm going to explode," with a big smile and the knowledge that her food was appreciated she said. "We wouldn't want you to do that Ranger"

With all the tension out of their conversation the two men settled back with a cup of coffee and a cigarette and started up a conversation about the Arnett's, and Sam agreed with Trudeau that they were extremely nice people. The one thing that Sam really appreciated from them was the fact that they say exactly what they thought and they said it in a way that you could not help but understand, plain and simple, straight to the truth, Mr. Arnett from what Sam had seen prided himself on saying what he meant, and meaning what he said!.

Suddenly Trudeau got a funny look in his face, and he blurted out. "Sam, let's go to the saloon and get a beer or two?" It didn't take a lot of prodding for Sam to answer "why not, sounds like fun, and this time we can ride our horses, you know, give them some exercise."

Trudeau just shook his head and said, "You just won't do son, you just won't do." With a chuckle, Sam answered, "I know, even when I was a kid I was always into something that I shouldn't be into, or up to something that would either get me extra chores or a whipping"!

Deciding that they were wasting time, the two men got up from the table, having already signed for the meal, they said goodnight to MS. Salazar and her daughter, then walked out the door, got on their horses and headed for the saloon. When they arrived in front of the saloon before getting down off of his horse. Sam checked his 45 to make sure it was fully loaded, and free in his holster. Trudeau seen what Sam was doing so he preceded to do the Sam

When they felt that they were prepared for any trouble that might come Sam and Trudeau walked into the saloon acting as if there was nothing wrong. Looking around after they had ordered a beer, they noticed the banker and the saloon owner coming out of the office and it seemed as if they were having a disagreement… about something. Trudeau looked over at Sam, and smiled. Then said, "Sounds just like an old married couple."

The two men decided that they were going to stick around for a while, so they found them a table back in the far corner and sat down, all this time keeping their eyes open and their ears turned to anything that they could hear. They had just finished their first beer when one of the saloon girls walked up to the table and ask if they wanted another, Sam nodded yes and told her to get one for herself.

"I hope you know what you're doing Sam, because if you don't, you might end up getting the girl hurt." "I know exactly what I'm doing, I seen this young lady talking to the owner and the banker so that tells me she was sent over here to find out what she could and report back to them, and you and I are going to give her all sorts of stuff to report back, and maybe it will screw them up enough and they'll make a mistake, what do you think Mr. Trudeau?"

Trudeau looked over at Sam and said, "Sounds like a plan to me, I just hope it works."

The longer they sat at the table, with the young lady. The more irritated the banker got, finally he got up and stormed out of the saloon and appeared to be headed back to the hotel. Sam didn't figure that it would take long for the saloon owner to call the girl away from the table, so Sam and Trudeau really started talking it up and accidentally on purpose letting a few details slip about the man they had locked up for murder and finding out who the man was associated with then, and who he is associated with now. The girl must have caught a sign from her boss, because she would be back before long to check them, when she left the table she went directly over to her bosses table and sat down. From the looks of things she was telling him everything that she had heard Sam and Trudeau talk about.

Sam very shyly looked at Trudeau and said, "Something is wrong, you need to go over to the jail and check on your prisoner. I don't see any of the four guards that are normally here, I've got a funny feeling Milliard and I don't like it."

Without saying anything except "order me another beer, I'll be right back" Trudeau went out the door and straight to the jail. He was only gone for a few minutes. When he returned to the saloon. He walked in and straight over to the table where Sam was sitting, picked up his beer and took a big long drink. Setting down he learned forward and said to Sam "all's well in the jail, the prisoner is asleep, and so is my deputy."

"Where are you spending the night tonight?" I'll sleep in my office tonight, as soon as I leave here, I will send my deputy home and he'll come back first thing in the morning to relieve me, so I can do whatever I have to do"

Sam looked at Trudeau, nodded his head, "I think I'm going to sleep over at the jail tonight myself."

Being that they still had a half a pot of coffee left, they decided to have a cigarette and another cup a coffee before calling it a night. Sam could tell by his actions that Trudeau was happy that Sam had decided to spend the night in jail with him.

Trudeau had noticed, there was something about Sam that when he got these feelings that he talks about, they come true. No longer than Trudeau had known Sam, he had learned that this Ranger had something very special. It was as if he could predict what was going to happen, and when it would occur. There was something on Sam's mind, he believed that something was going to happen, and it was going to happen tonight. They had finished off the pot of coffee and with nothing else left to eat or drink both men decided to head for the jail house and prepare for whatever was going to happen.

The two of them gathered up their horses and rode across Town to the Marshall's office. When they arrived they found the door to the office standing wide open, cautiously both men entered the jail, and instantly there came a voice, saying, "Stop right where you are and identify yourself." "It's me, Dustin, Trudeau and I got the Ranger with me! What the hell happened here?"

"There was four men who tried to brake in and wanted to free the prisoner, but after I've fired both barrels of this shotgun into the door, I guess they changed their minds, I'm glad they did because this shotgun took the door down and I didn't have any more shotgun shells close"

"Can you recognize these four men? " "Yes Sir, I sure can. It was the four men from the saloon that are employed as guards. I'm quite sure a couple of them has got double ought buck somewhere to in their bodies, maybe even some wood sprinters."

Trudeau told the deputy to go to the carpenters house wake him up and telling him we need a new door and we need it now, and on our way drop our horses off at the livery stable. After that he was to go home and get a good night's rest and be back at seven in the morning. Trudeau asked, Sam, "Do we go after them tonight? "No, if we go after them tonight, they'll just run, if we don't go after them they will think that Dustin couldn't identify them, and it will make it easier for us to get them when the saloon opens up tomorrow, can you get in touch with judge walker and get arrest warrants for those four men, and for Me. Wells. We need these warrants tonight so that we don't spend half the day tomorrow getting them. Four men I want him charged with attempted jailbreak and Mr. Wells for one count of attempted jailbreak and harboring a fugitive."

"Do you really think that you can make the changes against Wells stick?" Trudeau asked, "I don't know if I can get enough to get him jail time, but I am quite sure that I can prove enough to ask the judge to cancel his saloon license and order him out of town."

Doggone if that ain't the slickest way of getting rid of some very bad people, without having to empty a six shooter or a riffle at them to get their attention, personally I like being able to unload a shotgun in the direction of people like them."!!

CHAPTER 3

Sam decided while they were waiting on the carpenter, they might as well go ahead and take what was left of the door down that would make it easier on the carpenter hanging a new door. Besides Sam doubled that they would try again tonight.

Looking over at Trudeau Sam was surprised to see the man had fallen asleep, as if he didn't have a care in the world. Or maybe it was because he felt he had someone he could trust to watch his back. Sam just smiled and continued taking what was left of the jail house door down. He was in the process of separating what would was left still attached to the hinges when the carpenter pulled up on his wagon. Getting down he looked at Sam and said, "Have some kind of open house party tonight? Sure seems to have been a rowdy bunch." Then with a giggle. He said, "Come on Ranger and give me a hand with this door, when I built this jail house I kind of figured sooner or later, that I would need to hang another door so I made three, this is number two. I'll have it hung in just a little while. "Take your time, Sam said" no, sir, I can't do that. I left a willing woman at home in bed so I'm going to do this, just as fast I can. Then with another chuckle he started to work, and in no time at all, he had this door fitted bolts. In less than an hour the door was hung. He closed and opened the door three of four times adjusting on it each time until he felt that the door was perfect. He then turned to Sam and said, "Tell old sleepyhead there that I'll fill out the bill tomorrow and drop it off." With that he climbed aboard his wagon turned it around on Main Street, and headed back towards his house with a big smile on his face.

Sam kind of smile himself, knowing that this old man had something to look forward too, closing the door , Sam lit a lantern and sat down at Trudeau's desk and started going through Trudeau's wanted posters. There was one poster that seemed interesting, the man and his gang were all wanted for bank robbery and murder, the wanted poster was dated four months ago. It stated that he was wanted for robbery and murder in Kansas City, Wichita Oklahoma city and Abilene, Texas. It seemed that this Alan Klein was headed for El Paso. Sam thought to himself, "It might pay to keep an eye out for this man."

Sam got up, went over to Trudeau and nudged him, he woke up and Sam told him, "okay, sleeping beauty go in there and get in bed now, the door is fixed and its bolded from the inside, and the bar is in place, so the door can't be opened, and I'm going back here and get in one of the cells and go to sleep. I don't think they're going to try anything else tonight, but tomorrow is a different story.

With that Sam picked up the lantern that he had lit to read the wanted posters, and he headed back to the rear of the building, opened up a cell and made himself comfortable, the best that he could … and went to sleep.

Trudeau was awakened the next morning by the pounding on the door, he got up and looked out the window. It was his deputy, dusty. Walking over to the other window. Trudeau looked to make sure that Dusty was alone, after satisfying himself that there was no one else out there with dusty Trudeau opened the door and let him in, closing and barring the door behind him. He then directed dusty to go back and wake Sam up.

The deputy not knowing Sam very well found it smarter to speak loudly rather than go in the cell and touch him, which was the smart thing to do. He had to speak very loudly to Sam twice before he woke him up. Sam hadn't got his boots on yet. When another knock came on the door. Walking over and reluctantly looking out the window. Trudeau was satisfied that it was the delivery of food for the prisoner, so he opened the door once again and let him in. Placing the tray down on the desk. So Trudeau could go through it and make sure there was no weapons of any kind , the delivery man picked up the tray and took it back to the prisoner while Trudeau unlock the cell door and watched him as he handed the tray to the prisoner. Then he stepped back, Trudeau locked the cell door and said, "You can pick up that tray and the spoon when you bring his meal at lunch." The man smiled and said , "okay, now , will you let me out of here, I don't like of being locked up in this place, " Trudeau raise the bar off of the door and let the man out walking over to the water bucket he ladled up enough water to fill the coffee pot, put it on the stove then build a fire and sat down in his chair and leaned back, propping his feet up on the desk and he had not yet put on his boots.

Sam had managed to wake up and get his boots on. Walking into the main office, Sam told Trudeau, "I'm so hungry that I could eat just about anything, how about you, Trudeau?" The deputy spoke up "I've already had my breakfast, why don't you to go on down to the cantina and get yours. I'll take care of the coffee and make sure it doesn't boil away."

Trudeau looked at the deputy and said , you know the drill, don't open the door for anybody unless you know them, and they are alone , and then only if there is a damn good reason for them to want in this office." After we have our breakfast we'll be back and then if I'm not mistaken Ranger Cooper and I have a little job to perform this morning. Reaching into the inside pocket of his vest Trudeau pulled out five folded pieces of paper and handed them to Sam.

These were the warrants that Sam had asked Trudeau to get from judge walker. They were sworn to by United States marshal. Milliard Trudeau, and signed by federal judge, Boris Stephen walker. These warrants ordered Marshall Trudeau to arrest four men for attempted jailbreak and one man for harboring a fugitive and there was also written orders to close the gold nugget saloon.

Sam looked at Trudeau, shook his head and ask, "Do you think the two of us can handle it? Or do we need a couple more men that we can trust?" "As far as I can tell, there are four of us, "Trudeau said, "there is your deputy Manuel, there is dusty my deputy, if you don't think that is enough there is two more people that I can call on."

"No, I think that'll do it, if we do this quickly and take them by surprise, there should be a minimum of gunplay, but like I said we have to do it quickly as quite as possible. Four shotguns, along with their side arms.

Should be enough. After we get back from having our breakfast I want you to step on your horse and go to my office and get Manuel and bring him back down here. If we do this right, it should be over with pretty quickly, you got anything you want to add Trudeau? "Nope, seemed like everything is in pretty good shape, now if we can just keep from get killed, everything will be hunky- dory." "Well, I don't see any reason why we should take a chance on getting killed on an empty stomach, let's go get some chow, Sam said.

Acting as if there was nothing wrong. Trudeau and Sam headed for the cantina and they made it a point to be seen laughing and joking. As if they don't have a care in the world, as they were walking they kept an eye on the saloon and the second floor where Well's office was.

Trudeau looked over at Sam and said "Maybe it's a mite early for them to be stirring" "That's all right, Sam said, they'll be stirring before long, whether they like it or not.

Stepping into the cantina and once again setting down at a table in the corner, the waitress immediately brought over a pot of coffee and 2 cups. With a smile that seemed to light. Up the room she said, "Do you want a Mexican breakfast? Or do you want an American breakfast? "I don't care as long as there is a lot of it, Trudeau said" when she returned to leave Trudeau spanked her bottom, she immediately turned around, looked at Trudeau and said, "Don't start nothing that you can't finish gringo"

Sam said to Trudeau, "If I was you I wouldn't start nothing with that lady, she just might take you out behind the woodshed and teach you to keep your hands to your self-introducing you to a broom handle."

"If I didn't flirt with her when I come in her, I guarantee you that she would think something was wrong. We have gone through the same ritual for almost five, "no, almost 6 years now, it took me almost a year to get up the nerve to ask her what her name was" "Sam asked, what's her name?" ….. Trudeau, smiled and answered, "Rosa"

It wasn't very long till she came out carrying their breakfast, She had brought both of them the same thing. Smiling a big smile. "I felt like you really wanted an American breakfast. So here is an omelet with everything you can think of in it, some fried potatoes with onions and peppers in them, also some biscuits and gravy. Is there anything else I can get for you?"

Trudeau didn't say anything , so Sam spoke up, "No, Rosa I think you've got everything covered, thank you," When she walked away she had a funny look on her face, it seemed to upset her that Trudeau didn't talk back to her in flirty way.

Do you see what I mean now? She really expects me to flirt with her or teaser her Every time I come in here. It's just the way we have treated each other for so many years that now it's expected of me"

Dropping the subject, the two men started eating their breakfast. Then she came out of the kitchen, walked directly up to the table and said, "All right Mr. Trudeau, what's wrong with you? Are you upset with me about something? Or are you just being an ass? "Nothing's wrong, Rosa I was just proving a point"

Rosa then started in on Trudeau about using her to prove a point and she really let him have it, finally Trudeau stood up, took hold of her face with both hands and kissed her, Sam wasn't sure but he thought he felt the heat off of that kiss, when he turned loose of her she seemed dumbfounded, and Trudeau had a look on his face like the cat that ate the canary. Sam figured this was one of them times when he needed to keep his mouth shut, so he just kept right on eating.

Trudeau sat down and without saying a word about anything, he started eating and Sam could have sworn that Trudeau had a big smile on his face, and a sparkle in his eyes, but again he figured he'd better let it go.

Sam kept looking out the window and watching the saloon, he was waiting for the bartender to open up and then he and Trudeau was going over and sat down. Trudeau in the back, Sam in the front, he was going to send Manuel up the back staircase and dusty was going to be outside at the first window. Until then, it was kind of a cat and mouse game to see who would be forced to move first. But either way it went Mr. Wells and his four hunch men weren't not going to be in business at the end of this day.

Finally Trudeau started talking, "Sam, why don't we just go over there and bust the door down and go in?" Sam answered, "what if, for some reason, the four men are not in there, what do we do then? We need those four to prove W

Wells is guilty, so we can pulled his permit and put him out of business."

"So this is one of them times where the law just has to sit and wait and let the bad guys hang themselves, so to speak."

"That's just about the size of it, "Sam said. Trudeau frowned just a little bit and said, "But Sam my way is so much more enjoyable," then he laughed and took a big drink of his coffee and began rolling him a cigarette.

"It's a shame that the saloon will be closed down, I'm going to miss sitting in there and drinking a beer." Trudeau said.

"It won't be closed for long Trudeau, I understand that the bartender has expressed. A willingness to buy the place from Wells, but so far Wells has been reluctant to talk about selling the place, but I think that's going to change!"

Trudeau and Sam had decided that they were going to clean up El Paso, and make it a City to be proud of. Where a woman can walk down the street without an escort and still not be accosted by some drunk cowboy or some tinhorn.

Sam had just poured himself another cup of coffee when he noticed that the bartender was opening up, but he still hadn't seen the four men, he was looking for, and until he did…. He had to stay put!

Trudeau went to poured himself another cup of coffee and there wasn't any, so he turned around and motion to Rosa and pointed to the coffee pot, she smiled and nodded her head yes. It wasn't but just a few minutes until she showed up with a fresh pot, and when she turned to walk away, she anticipated Trudeau and jumped out of his reach, then laughed.

Sam's plan was as soon as the four men went in to the saloon, they would spring their trap before any patrons had time to get in the way. So just as soon as these four men were sited they would spring into action and take them down. Hopefully they would catch them off guard enough that there wouldn't be any gunplay, this is what Sam hoped, but it's turning out that way was a long shot. These men hired their guns out and the only thing that would stop them from using their guns…. Was a bullet.

Sam and Trudeau were deep into conversation when Manuel and dusty walked in and came directly over to the table and sat down. Each man was carrying two shotguns. Manuel handed Sam a shotgun, checked it to see if it was loaded, it was , but Manuel handed Sam four more shells , "anyway" Dusty did the same to Trudeau, then he turned around and mentioned to Rosa to bring a couple of cups. So they could have a cup of coffee also.

Rosa brought out two extra cups and a tray full of homemade Cinnamon rolls, she then said , I would like for you gentlemen to try these, I'm thinking about starting to serve them, and I need to know if you think they're tasty enough, so eat all of them that you want, just let me know what you think, okay"

Picking one up Trudeau said, "Damn, these things are sticky", then he took a bite, and shook his head, saying, "By gum, they may be sticky, but they're sure are good, and even better with a hot cup of coffee. Rosa, think you got a winner." Everyone at the table agreed with Trudeau, they were quite tasty and as Trudeau said, even tastier when chased with a good cup of coffee.

Sam just happened to glance at the front of the saloon and he seen the four men go in. "Manuel, make your way to the rear of the saloon go up the back stairway and if you can't get through the door go through a window, I'll give you five minutes, then were going to close in. Dusty you make your way to the little walkway between the saloon and the barbershop. Trudeau, you go in first, pick a table signal me and I will make my way through the front door and I'll stop at the corner of the bar. This way we should have every angle covered. Oh Manuel if you happen to see Wells put a gun on him and bring him out onto the balcony with you."

Manuel was the first to leave, then Dusty, then Trudeau. Sam watched out the window as the three men took up their positions. Dusty was the only one he could see, so far right now. Dusty had to be Sam's eyes.

Seeing Manuel disappear behind the building, Sam, estimated that he had been gone about three minutes, so he got up and walked to the front door of the restaurant. Glancing over at Dusty, the deputy shook his head yes and Sam started for the saloon. When he walked into the saloon the four men they were after, were seated at a table drinking a beer and playing poker. Stopping at the end of the bar. He ordered a beer, and waited for Manuel to appear on the balcony, with or without Wells. When the bartender brought Sam his beer, he told the bartender in a very soft ice. "When you see me pick this shotgun up you hit the floor behind that bar and you stay down until I tell you to get up."

Manuel appeared on the balcony and in front of him was Wells, Sam picked up his shotgun pointed it at the four men and said, "Put your hands on the table and keep them there, don't try anything, you're covered four ways.

The four men didn't seem to be raffled at all, because one of them asked, "What's the charges Ranger? We haven't done anything, "Sam answered" the charges here in El Paso right now are attempted. Jailbreak and before you ask me if I have proof, stand up and take your shirts off, anyone of you who doesn't have buckshot wounds. Or wounds caused by flying wood can pick up your horses and ride out of town with the understanding that you not come back." Reluctantly, the four men took off their shirts, two of them had wounds that were bandaged up, and two of them had wounds from buckshot. Keeping his shotgun leveled on the table Sam walked over relieve the men of their side arms.

" Here's the choice you have, you can go to jail and be tried for attempted jailbreak or you can tell me who hired you, talk and you can get on your horses and ride out here with the understanding that you don't come back."

Wells hollered, "You men keep your mouth shut." When he said that Manuel nudged him with the barrel of the shotgun right in the small of his back and then said, "Señor the best thing you can do is to be quite."

Sam reached in his pocket and pulled out four pieces of paper and laid them on the table. The men looked down at the pieces of paper and only needed to see one word, "Warrant". The taller of the men asked, "we talk, and we ride, is that the deal!?"

"that's the deal," Sam answered, "well, I'm not into going to jail for somebody else or doing somebodies time for them, Wells paid us $100 a piece to get lane out of jail, but when your deputy fired that shotgun through the door all of us got hit with either wood splinters or buckshot , is that all , you need Ranger?"

"Yeah, that's all I need, now pick up your pistols, one at a time, gentlemen, and empty them, leave the shells on the table and get out. Remember do not come back because these warrants will still be in effect but they will only be served if you stop foot back inside the city limits."

Manuel spoke up and ask, "What should I do with Mr. Wells, Ranger?

"Bring him down here, Sam said" Manuel nudged him again in the small of the back with his shotgun and said, "You heard the ranger, move."

Sam could tell that Wells was not liking the way things was going. But he didn't really care about whether the ma. Liked things or not. Because he was really going to be upset when Sam showed him the warrant. Mr. Wells stood in front of Sam defiantly and said, "If you're trying to scare me Ranger you're not succeeding.

He's not trying to scare you, he's just going to make sure that you leave town, pronto." Trudeau said Sam looked over at the bartender and ask him, "Just how much stock would you say is in this place?" "I would say no more than $1500 worth, and that includes the poker tables, all of whiskey in the back room and the beer." the bartender answered. "Do you still want to buy this place?" "Yes sir, I do." "Do you have $1500? Sam asked" the bartender shook his head yes, "I've been saving money ever since I started work here." "Do you have your money in the bank across the street? Sam asked. "If you do, then I suggest you get over there and get it out of that bank, because I don't think it's going to be very long before that bank gets robbed.

Wells spoke up and said, "You can't force me to sell my saloon." "You might as well sell it because as of right now it's shut down, and because of criminal conduct all proceeds are confiscated, that means Mr. Wells that the only money you have is the money that is in the bank, what is in the till, along with all the stocks in the building are also confiscated, now if you want to sell this place to your bartender you can come up with $1500 cash plus what you have in the bank should give you enough money to set up somewhere else. It's your choice, Mr. Wells! What do you want to do? Manuel Mr. Wells doesn't seem to want to read the charges in person."

There is no need in doing that," Wells said. "Just have the bartender fill out a bill of sale and I'll sign it when he hands me $1500,"

Looking over at the bartender, Sam said. " if I was you I would get over to the bank right now and pull out whatever you're going to need to start running this place, because Mr. Wells will be on the evening stage, going somewhere, so if you're going to buy this bar, you need to do it now or it will be shut down permanently."

Like a shot the bartender was out the front door, almost at a run as he headed for the bank. In the meantime Wells was filling out a bill of sale in this handwriting, so there could be no discussion about the sale of the business. The bartender was back in no time at all $1500 in $20 gold pieces. Sam kind of that bag was, did you?"

Mr. Wells had his $1500. The bartender, Mr. Clark had his bill of sale witnessed by Milliard Trudeau and Samuel Cooper, Sam smiled at Wells and then told dusty and Manuel to escort him to the hotel and help him pack his belongings and see to it that he was on the next stage, leaving town.

When Wells had left the saloon. Mr. Clark banged on the bar and said, "gentlemen, when I came to work this morning, I was a little bit down because of the way things were going here, I never in my life thought that when this day ended I would be a businessman and I owe it to the four of you, I don't know how I can repay you, but I do know that I have the authority to buy you a beer. How about it, gentlemen, would you care to have the honor of having the first beer. How about it, gentlemen, would you care to have the honor of having the first beer on Bob Clark in this new establishment by the name of, the sage brush saloon."

"If you'll excuse me, gentlemen, I have to talk to the ladies and make sure that they are still going to work here, and I think I can fix it so that they make more money working for me than they did working for Wells."

"I don't see any reason why that they would want to go anywhere else, I imagine this is the first time in their lives that they have worked for an honest man. My advice to you, Mr. Clark is take care of business and keep it clean, the whiskey , not watered down, and the beer as cold as you can get it." "Trudeau spoke up and said, "Especially make sure the beer is cold." "I can tell already that there's going to be a big change in this section of El Paso, and personally I am looking forward to it, " came a voice from behind Sam and Trudeau , it turned out to be Lilian, I think I speak for all the ladies when I say, thanks,"!

Sam and Trudeau followed dusty and Manuel as they escorted Mr. Wells to his hotel room, and watched him gather up his belongings. Then escorted him to the bank where he drew out all of the money he had in the bank, much to Mr. Gordon's surprise, then he was escorted to the stage office. The noon stage going to Las Cruces, in the New Mexico territory was on time for a change. The two deputies pitched Mr. Wells belongings up on top of the stagecoach where the shotgun rider tied it down, then one deputy opened the stage door and motioned for him to get in, when he did Manuel closed the door, still carrying his shot gun, smiled at Mr. Wells and wished him a good trip.

Dusty turned around and looked at Manuel, Sam, and Trudeau and ask, "Now, can we all go have that good cold beer that Mr. Clark promised us?"

"I don't see any reason why we can't , we have pretty much taken care of the criminal elements on this side of town, with the exception of Mr. Gordon's bank, which is next on the list of people to leave this time. "Trudeau said.

Going back over the saloon, they could hear what sounded like a New Year's Eve party going on inside the saloon. When they walked into the saloon they received a standing ovation. They were just about to drink to the new owner of the sage brush saloon, when a tall, lanky man walked up to Trudeau and Sam and said, "I take it you're the law in this town, I'm from Abilene, Texas, and I'm here to pick up a man that you have in jail, here is the extradition order and the wanted poster And here's my badge. The Judge in Abilene said, if you have any doubts send him a wire"

"The stage just left, so are you plan on sending the night?" "No Sir, I'm not, were going to be talking the train tonight, so I need to get him out of the jail, and into chains then down to the train depot as soon as possible."

Dusty spoke up and said, "Marshall you and Sam go ahead and finish your beer. You've earned it, I'll escort this gentleman over to the jail and help him get the prisoner ready to go, then I'll be back for my beer."

Trudeau told Dusty, "You know the paperwork that has to be signed, so make sure it gets signed, especially the release papers releasing lane into this gentlemen's custody. By the way, Sir, what is your name?"

Pushing back his hat, he smiled and said, "I am Rusty Thompson, Texas ranger to be assigned to Abilene, Texas," "Sam spoke up and said, I've heard that name from Ben Johnson and he speaks very highly of you."

"Now it's your turn, what's your name?" "I'm united states Marshall Trudeau, and this is Sam Cooper, Texas Ranger assigned to El Paso, Texas. The other two gentlemen you met, one was my deputy, dusty, the other was Sam's Deputy Manuel, two extremely good men."

"Thanks for the beer, gentlemen, but I really need to get the prisoner and get going. If you're ever in my neck of the woods stop by and see me and I promise you, I'll treat you to a beer, so long my friends." Without saying another word the ranger turned and walked out of the saloon, by now Dusty should have all the paperwork ready for him to sign, all they needed now was to get the prisoner to the train station.

Manuel followed the Ranger out of the saloon and ask him, "I take it, Sir, that you are going to need another horse in order to get him to the train station, is that not so," the Ranger just shook his head and Manuel continued, "there are two horses tied in front of the Marshall's office. I'm quite sure that we can borrow them long enough to get your man to the train station, and I will bring back the empty horse. I take it you are going to board your horse on the train?"

"That's exactly what I intended to do, Manuel, Are you sure that your boss will not mind?"

"You know your self-Ranger that in our line of work there is never anything absolute, but I am quite sure that neither the Marshall or the Ranger will mind if we use their horses, besides those horses need the exercise, I heard Sam say so"

When the Ranger walked into the Marshall's office, he found the papers already filled out and on the Marshall's desk ready to be signed. The prisoner was seated in a chair he had a waist chain on, one end of a set of leg irons attached to a pair of handcuffs, the other end was attached to his leg, right above the ankle. This would enable him to set straddle of a horse, but not be able to run.

Looking at Lane, and seeing how he was chained the Ranger ask, "Who taught you how to be chain like that? Ranger Sam, he taught me never to give these men the opportunity to attack you, because they will the minute you let guard down. Manuel is going to escort you down to the train depot, whenever you're ready and bring back the horse that Lane is going to have to ride." Then Dusty stuck out his hand in a gesture of friends and said, "You keep your eyes on this man, because he will kill you if he gets the chance, my advice to you is, do not remove the chain going to his handcuffs, no matter what."

The Ranger shook Dusty's hand, looked at Manuel and said, "Let's get this show on the road, I don't want to have spent any more time with this man than I have to, I think it's going to take about 36hours on the train and that means no sleep for me, unless there is someone there that I trust to watch this man."

"If you don't mind the company sir, I would be more than glad to help you get this man back to Abilene." "I'm not sure that the Marshall would let you do that," "I think he will because we don't have any prisoners for him to watch, if you hold on for just a minute, I'll go ask him."

Dusty came into the saloon walked directly up to the Marshall, then he explained what he had in mind, also explaining that they had no prisoners for him to watch and being that he was a part-time deputy, all he needed was a train ticket to Abilene and back. Trudeau agreed with him and told him, "Take whatever he needed out of petty cash and have Manuel bring back the two extra horses to the Marshall's office. And when you start back from Abilene send a wire and let him know what time you will arrive, that way he can have someone at the train station with a horse, so you won't have to walk back into town."

Nodding his head in acceptance, dusty turned and headed back to the Marshall's office. When he walked back in the Marshall's office, he went directly to his desk and counted out $30, Then Said, "let's go or we're going to Miss that train."

With nothing else left to say the Ranger got hold of the chain around lanes waste and led him out to a horse and helped him aboard, all this time Dusty was holding on the bridal of lanes horse. He continued holding on to the bridal until Thompson was in the saddle on his horse, and he and Manuel followed Thompson and Lane out of town.

When they reached the train station, Manuel never dismounted, but instead dusty handed him the reins to both horses. The two men started at each other for just a moment then dusty stuck out his hand and Manuel took it and said, " be extremely careful, my friend, we need you in this town to help clean it up" "only the devil himself will keep me from coming back , this I promise, " Dusty said.

Dusty and Thompson and Lane stood watching Manuel as he slowly headed back to town, when he had gone 100 yards he turned and waved at one old friend, and one new friend, then he turned and never looked back,

Arriving back in town Manuel tied not only his horse, but Sam's horse and Marshall's to the hitching post in front of the Marshall's office, and feeling an emptiness he turned and walked across the street to the saloon. He felt he needed to have a drink in honor of his old friend.

As Manuel stepped up the bar Sam could tell something was bothering him so he asked, "What's on your mind, Manuel?" "I just have a feeling Sir, an empty feeling about dusty going with this Ranger, I fear there is going to be trouble," "Do you think if you were there with him that things would be different?" "Yes Sir, I do." Then Sam pointed his finger at Manuel and said, "then what in the hell are you doing here, here's $20 gold pieces get back out there to that train and help Dusty delivered that prisoner." There was a light that came into Manuel's eyes and smile came across his face and all he said was, "May the gods always smile on you, my friend," still carrying that double barrel shotgun Manuel leaped up on his horse and went out of town at a dead run.

Sam looked over at Trudeau, and made a gesture with his shoulders, "Do you think we can get somebody to go out to the depot and pick up Manuel's horse?"

Trudeau chuckled just a little and said" don't worry about it Sam, I'll get somebody to do it, or do it myself. We have two mighty fine deputies, you and I should both be thankful for these two men,"

"I swear right now Trudeau, that if anything happens to either one of those deputies I will not rest until who ever harms them is brought back here and punished to the full extent of the law." Sam swore this in front of everyone in the saloon.

Figuring it was time to get something to eat. Sam asked Trudeau if he would like to join him for either an early supper or a late lunch. Trudeau answered by saying, "Don't mind if I do, but today it's on me! Sam, smiled and said "well, all right"

Sam and Trudeau left the saloon and started to walk, then Sam realized the hammerhead was still tied to the railing in front of the Marshall's office. So he decided he was going to ride instead if walk. Trudeau said. "what the hell I got to come back this way too, both men walked across the street got on their horses, and led the third horse with them to the livery stable and dropped it off. Then they preceded up the street into miss Salazar's for a good meal, and then maybe a good night's sleep in their own bed, in their own room , in the hotel, Mrs. Salazar seemed shocked to see Trudeau and Sam she asked, "is anything wrong? Is everything all right with the two deputies? Why aren't they with you?

Sam said. "Whoa, ma'am, one question at a time, no, yes, their gone out of town." She then looked at Sam." I guess I did get a little overbearing, but I worry so much about the four of you."

Trudeau finally spoke up and said, "That's all right. Consuela, it's just been a long time since any of us has had anybody that cared enough to worry, I guess we've forgotten how it feels. I'll tell you what, we'll try not to worry you, if you will promise to always care about us. "Trudeau dropped his head as Consuela went back to the kitchen, she had to because what Trudeau had said made her cry and that made Trudeau sad.

"Don't take it so hard Milliard, those aren't tears of sadness, those are tears of happiness you just made that ladies day. I think she now feels that all four of us are part of her family, one really is, and she has three stepsons."

Just sitting there looking out the window Sam was wondering about Dusty and Manuel and Ranger Thompson, he believed that this would be a good experience for the two deputies, it would not only raise their self-esteem, but it would also let them know that they are trusted to be able to do any job they are asked to do, Allowing those two deputies to assist in the transporting of a killer, such as Lane could, and should, be a turning point in these two young men lives, and maybe it was time that they became full-time deputies. He would have to speak to Trudeau about making it happen for Dusty and he would speak to Ms. Salazar about making it happen for Manuel.

He was brought back to reality when Trudeau, all but hollered at him, "Sam, are you okay?" "Of course I'm okay, why do you ask?" "I asked, because Consuela has been trying to get your attention, so she could set your food down in front of you,"

Sam realized that he had been off in Lalaland again, so he apologized to Consuela by saying, "I'm sorry Ms. Salazar, but I've got something I want to ask you and I am worried about what your answer might be, so here goes, Ms., Salazar is it all right with you if I offer Manuel a full time job as my deputy?" Believe it or not, Ms. Salazar seemed relieve when she heard the question that Sam wanted to ask her, when Sam seen the expression on Ms. Salazar's face. He then realized that he had started the question out wrong, and that he had actually scared Ms. Salazar, he then asked her, "Miss Salazar were you afraid I was going to ask you for your hand?" "It crossed my mind, but I knew that your question was taken out of context, now listen to me, you've got me talking with those big words like you do when you're trying to make point. To be very bluntly I would turn you down Sam Cooper, because I never want to be married again."

There wasn't much talking going on, just a lot of eating. It seemed that doing their job created an appetite, or maybe it was knowing that they had indeed with their actions today started cleaning up El Paso and making it a place that you can be proud to call home. Whatever the case. Sam and Trudeau was eating as if they hadn't eaten in a week or two. For some reason today the food just seemed to be exceptionally flavorful.

Pushing back from the table Sam began to roll him a cigarette and of course, Trudeau pulled out a cigar, Trudeau always said that a cigar after a meal enhanced the meal two fold, that was just about the way that Sam felt about a cigarette after a good meal. So both of these law men settled back in their chairs with a cup of coffee in one hand and a smoke in the other, and started discussing what their next move was going to be concerning Mr. Gordon and the bank, it was quite obvious that it wouldn't going to be as easy as Mr. Wells was, but still, it had to be done.

After talking turns sleeping, Ranger Thompson, along with Dusty and Manuel had made it through the night without any kind of incident concerning Lane. It had come time for the prisoner to eat, so Thompson decided that all four men should sit at the same table and eat. Dusty and Manuel were like a couple of kids on their first train ride, they were really enjoy their new found freedom, and the opportunity to be more than just a jailer, both young men felt like they had graduated and had become real, true to life law men . It was plain to see that neither one of these men would do anything to put his new feeling in jeopardy. The one thing that both men agreed on was that they needed to do a really good job for Ranger Thompson and the delivery of the prisoner in one piece, and in good health to the Texas Rangers stationed in Abilene, Texas,

The train had moved along steadily, except for stopping to take on water and wood every hundred miles or so. Ranger Thompson explained to Dusty and Manuel that Lane was known member of a gang headed by Alan Klein. For the past year him and his gang had terrorized North Central Texas, and were now moving into western Texas, and possibly southeastern New Mexico territory. It was clear that it made Ranger Thompson mad when he had to reveal that when Klein crossed over into New Mexico territory that he had no authority to pursue him, and that it had to be done by United States Marshall's. It was a standing thing that any time one of Klein's gang was caught he would rob a bank and kill several people just to be doing it.

The last bank that he robbed, he not only killed the owner and two tellers, but after collecting all of the money, silver and gold. He preceded to burn the bank to the ground, and made sure that everyone knew it was because one of this gang had been tried, convicted, and hung.

Hearing this story, Dusty and Manuel were anxious to get back to town, because it seemed that Klein's gang was headed toward El Paso. This was their home and it was their job to protect it against all corners. Manuel and Dusty made up their mind that they would escort the prisoner to the jail House in Abilene and then immediately go back to the train station to catch the next train back to El Paso. Both men felt that they had been away from their duties in town for far too long, and they felt the tension of not being there to back up Sam and Trudeau.

CHAPTER 4

Sam woke up the next morning feeling as if a great weight had been lifted from his shoulders, and it was a feeling that Sam had not felt in a long time. It really felt good to be back at miss Salazar's boarding house's staying in the hotel was fine, but there was just something about this little boarding house that made Sam feel at home and it was a good feeling.

This morning, Sam was up and dressed before the knock came on his door and instead of answering, he just opened the door and stepped into the dining room and the first thing he asked was "do you mind if I sit down at the table now and have a cup of coffee?"

No Sam, we do not mind at all." Came a voice from the back of the kitchen. It was Ms. Salazar and she was preparing to put the food on the table and as usual it took in the appearance of a feast. As she placed the food on the table she told Sam to go ahead and dig in. Instead of filling his plate. He looked up at Miss Salazar and smiled. Then said, "If it's alright with you, ma'am, I would just as soon wait on everybody else, besides I have nothing really pressing today. There are no prisoners in either jail, and since Mr. Clark took over the saloon, there has been no fights or anyone locked up for public drink." Looking at the food on the table Sam said. "Ms. Salazar I really feel sorry for Marshall Trudeau. He doesn't get to sit down at a table like this first thing in the morning and taste the best cooking in town, I don't know if I've ever said it before, but I will say it now, Thank you, ma'am, for allowing me to sit at this table with you and your family."

She spoke up very quickly and said, Samuel Cooper, if you start me crying again I will smack you, now hush and eat your breakfast." Glancing over at Ms. Salazar's daughter she had a smile on her face and she moved her lips forming the words "Thank you" Then she pointed at his plate and said very sternly, "eat"!

Deciding that he had best nit upset these two ladies, he preceded to fill his plate and start eating. By the time the others had got to the table Sam was just about done eating breakfast and he said to the others, "sorry about starting before you got to the table, but it's an early morning for me, I've been laying off of my paperwork for so long it will probably take me two days to get caught up, Then he looked at Ms. Salazar, smiled and winked. He then asked to be excused, but before leaving he reached and got a biscuit and a piece of ham and made himself a ham biscuit to take to the office with him. Ms. Salazar filled up a large cup with steaming hot coffee and said, take this with you. I know there's no one at the Ranger station to make coffee, so this should tide you over until you get some made" "thank you, ma'am, it will surely hit the spot and go quite well with this ham biscuit, besides I want Trudeau to know what he's missing, maybe I can get him to start staying here too, that is if you think you can stand him."

It was such a pretty day that Sam decided to stop by the livery stable and asked the man who worked there to keep his horse handy just in case he needed to get him saddled quickly, but he could see no sense in the horse having to stand in front of the Rangers office all day. After conversing with poppa mike, at the livery stable. Sam preceded on his way to the Rangers office to take care of the stuff that Manuel would take care of if he was here. When Sam turned the corner a half a block from the Rangers office, he noticed a horse tied to the hitching post in front. No one was supposed to be in that office at this hour. Stopping before he got to the front door. He peaked through the window in front and got a huge surprise. There sitting at his desk with his feet propped up and his hat pulled down over his eyes was Ben Johnson.

Opening the door and making as much noise as possible, Sam stepped inside and said, "it's good to see you Ben, but if you need to go to sleep. There's a cot just down the hall on the right."

"Not here on a social call Sam, I'm here to warn you that Alan Klein and his bunch is headed this way and their leaving a trail of dead people and robbed banks. The last account we had of him. He was somewhere in the neighborhood of Abilene, Texas, then all of a sudden him and his bunch just seemed to drop out of sight, I was told to authorize you to hire at least two more deputies for your own safety. This man and his bunch are stone cold killers, they don't care how old or young, male or female that you are if you pose a threat to them in any way they will kill you and never bat an eye."

"Where are you headed from here Ben?" Sam asked. "I'm supposed to take the southern route down to Laredo and then back up to Austin, that should take me just about the rest of the year, They don't want me to take a train or stagecoach, because I might cross their trail and never know it, You take care of yourself Sam, and remember what I taught you keep your eyes and your ears open and your mouth shut. "He then stuck out his hand, Sam took it with the film grip that Ben had taught him always to shake with.

Ben was never one for making long speeches, hell, he was never one to talk very much at all. So Sam felt very lucky that the man thought enough of him to come by and deliver the message about Klein and tell him to careful and alert at all times. So Sam was surprised when Ben put both hands on Sam's shoulders and said, "You have been like a son to me ever since the day that your family died, and I could not be prouder than I am right now"!!

Without saying anything else, Ben walked out the door, swung up on his horse, waved goodbye, turned his horse and never looked back. Sam stood on the walkway and watched Ben until he was completely out of sight.

When Sam went back into the office and sat down at his desk, he began to get a worried look on his face. Ben Johnson would not have come all this way, if there was not a legitimate worry. Been always said that when "danger" comes calling, "hell" comes with him. Sam was sitting at his desk going through his wanted posters when Trudeau walked in, without any hesitation at all Sam told Trudeau what Ben had told him, all Trudeau would say was he sure did wish that dusty and Manuel would get back here pretty quick, just in case.

The train slowly came to a stop in Abilene, when it had come to a complete stop Ranger Thompson stepped off of the train and glanced around to make sure there was no welcoming party, then motioned for Dusty and Manuel bring the prisoner off of the train. Ranger Thompson then told the two deputies to go get them a beer and a good meal, it would help them kill the next two hours till the westbound train pulled in and they could start back. He'd thanked them for their assistance, filled out a chit so that they would be paid for their time. He then shook their hands and escorted Lane to the jail house, which was only a couple of buildings down.

Dusty and Manuel seen a saloon just down the street on the left that had a sign stating that they had good food, so both men decided a beer and a steak, we go pretty good right now. But first they had to find the telegraph office and send a telegram to Sam or the Marshall telling them they had delivered the prisoner and was headed back. It was a good feeling to both young man to know that they had completed a very important job without incident. They were beginning to feel the pride that made Sam and Trudeau stand out, and they were beginning to understand that although respect was given to the badge. That same respect a man had to be earned.

After finding the telegraph office and taking care of business, the two young deputies preceded to the saloon, and a well-earned beer and a steak. As they entered the saloon, they noticed that there was only two cowboys standing at the bar, the rest of the place was empty, not thinking too much of it at the time the young men preceded to a table and sat down. A pretty young redhead made her way over to the table, smiled and said, "what can I do for you cowboys" then she noticed the badge is on their chest and the two deputies could tell that it made her extremely nervous, so Manuel speaking very softly asked her, "what's wrong?" Acting as if she was taking their orders she told them the two men standing at the bar was part of the Klein gang.

Manuel told the saloon girl to go on back in the kitchen and get their order and not to worry. She turned and went to the bar and got two beers returned to the table and set them down and said their steaks would be ready in short order, then turned and went back into the kitchen. Manuel and Dusty, then downed their beers and got up carrying the empty mugs and preceded to the bar, giving the impression that they were going to get two more beers. When they got close to the two men standing at the bar, both Dusty and Manuel drew their Colt's and told the two men not to move a muscle, Then they reached and disarmed the two men, the Manuel told one of the men to put his hands on the edge of the bar and take one good step back. Dusty following Manuel's lead done the same with the other man, and then while Manuel held a gun on them Dusty checked to see if they were carrying any other kind of weapons. Both men were carrying knives and one was carrying another small pistol tucked underneath his gun belt.

Having been taken completely by surprise had irritated the two men to the extent that they started making threats, one man said, " Klein is not going to like this, he does not like this men messed with and you have just bit off a whole lot more than you can chew." Smiling Manuel looked at the man and said, "We weren't really sure that you were members of Klein's gang before, but thanks to you running off at the mouth… we are now."! "Tell that pretty young redhead

Will be right back, we have to take these two men over to the jail house, and by the way, draw us another beer, if you don't mind. Ranger Thompson seemed quite surprised when the two deputies came through the front door and said, "here's two more members of Klein's gang, we weren't really sure who they were until this big mouth feller right here started shooting off his mouth and making threats, would you believe that he actually admitted to being part of Klein's gang, he even told us that we were biting off more than we could chew. So we kind of figured we should introduce them to you."

Thompson had a big smile on his face as he walked back into the jail house, unlocked two cell doors and said" welcome to your temporary home, gentlemen, the judge will see you shortly." He then turned around and locked at the two deputies, "maybe I should just keep you two around here, you can make my job a whole lot easier, he'll, you don't even have to go chase the bad guys, and they just come up and introduce themselves to you."

Dusty spoke up this time and said, "Thanks, but no thanks, we have got two of the best bosses that there ever was back in El Paso and as soon as we eat our supper we're going to be heading for that train. We've already sent a telegram telling them that were on our way back. So no offense Ranger, but we think we'll stick with what we got."

Turning very abruptly both deputies were out the door and headed back to the saloon. When they walked back in the saloon. The redhead saloon girl was standing at the end of the bar, the moment she seen them. She hot footed it back to the kitchen and before they got to their table she came out if the kitchen carrying two Platters containing a large T-bone steak, and fried potatoes. The bartender was right behind her with two large beers and a plate that had four large rolls on it. They placed the food and drinks down on the table said thanks, this is on the house and left the two deputies alone.

They weren't really sure how much time they had before the westbound train would be pulling in, so they focused on the task of getting all of this food eaten before that train pulled in. It was a good thing that they decided to take care of the food before doing a lot of talking because they had no sooner finished their steaks than they heard the whistle in the distance, so they downed their beers and Manuel dropped a $20 gold piece on the table and told the bartender, "that should cover our meal, and the beers, and I expect that young lady to get her share of what's left over." The bartender smiled, "as far as I'm concerned she can have it all, if it hadn't been for her those two men would still be here and I don't know about you but to me that's nit funny."

The two men only said, "We got to go." And they bolted out the front door headed back to the train depot, which thank god was not very far away, so they were standing on the platform when the train pulled in. They had already gotten their tickets and were eager to get in the train, getting back to El Paso and familiar surrounding seem to be the only thing that was on these two deputies minds.

Dusty turned to Manuel and said, "This has been the most exciting thing that has ever happened to me, but I've enjoyed all of this that I can stand. It is going to feel so good to get back to El Paso."!

Sam and Trudeau were working together going through all of the new wanted posters when the young boy who worked as a runner for the telegraph office came through the front door and handed Trudeau a telegram. Opening it, Trudeau said, "It's from our long-lost deputies. They have delivered that prisoner in Abilene and are back on the train headed home, says here, they should be here about 11 o'clock tomorrow night. Well I guess we'll have to get their horses out and meet them."

"Why don't we just get a buckboard from the livery Sam asked?"

"I never was much of a hand at driving a buck board, can you drive one?" Laughing, Sam said, "I cut my teeth on the buckboard, when I was about nine years old. I used to drive the wagon when we gathered corn or stacked hay, anything that needed a buckboard, it was my job to drive it. I don't think through the years that I have forgotten how"

It was getting close to suppertime so Sam asked "Trudeau if he would like to join him for supper at miss Salazar's boarding house? Trudeau answered by saying, "I got a better idea Sam, let me buy your supper at the cantina. I understand that young lady that waited on us the other night entertains by doing one of those fancy Mexican dances after dark,"

"Okay, Sam said, but beer only tonight no tequila. "Trudeau, smiled and said, "That I can agree with, wholeheartedly. I am not really over the other night, yet. Besides, they do have the coldest beer in town. It sure is going to feel good to have those two deputies back in town again, didn't think I would, but I miss Dusty, he's a very well raised young man that has a lot of potential, and I'm going to hire full time when he gets back."

"you remember what I told you that Ben Johnson told me that I was authorized to hire me a couple of extra deputies, so I'm going to hire Manuel and I think I'll asked Luis if he'd be interested, besides I don't speak Spanish, as well as I should, and with these two around, I should learn pretty quickly, don't you think?"

Trudeau got up, stretched, looked at Sam and motioned for him to come on. Sam locked up the Ranger station and left a note on the door that he would either be at the cantina or at Ms. Salazar's boarding house if anyone needed him.

It took the better part of a half hour to get to the cantina, mainly because everyone that Sam and Trudeau met wanted to talk for a spell, and being a public servant they both were courteous enough to spend a few minutes with each one. Listening to people's problems, or getting their input on a problem has always been something that law men has had to accept from the community, and more often than not the advice that some of the people give you is good advice, but most of the time their problems are not something that can be settled by the law. A lot of their problems can be settled by simply sitting down and talking as a group to a padre.

That is something Sam never had any problem with mainly because a padre cannot solve a problem when the problem is someone shooting at you. Up till now that is the only problem that Sam had. He didn't have a girlfriend to get in trouble with, the saloon girl was already spoken for, and so was the wait at the cantina, It seemed that every woman in town was spoken for with the exception of Ms. Salazar's oldest daughter. That was a

Direction that Sam was not willing to go into, simply because he respected Ms. Salazar that much, there was no way a woman of her beauty would want anything to do with a plain ordinary man with plain ordinary looks like Sam. To even think about her was just the same as daydreaming, and daydreaming was not a luxury that Sam could afford to do,

Trudeau looked over at Sam and ask, "Okay Sam. You got that look on your face again, what's on your mind?

"Sorry, Trudeau, you caught me daydreaming and I'm not supposed to do that." "Why not, Sam? You're a young, vigorous young man that has hopes and dreams just like anyone else, so give me one good reason why you shouldn't dream about having a woman of your own?"

"I had another dream the other night and it was pretty much the same as the first dream. I believe Milliard, that in the near future, it's going to end for me, and I cannot take the chance of leaving a woman, and maybe a child to survive on their own, it's just wouldn't be right. I have pretty much given into the idea that I'm going to die, I believe in my dreams, Milliard, I always have and always will. Remember what I'm telling you, because what I'm telling you, because it is going to happen …and soon!

Trudeau had a worried look on his face and instead of trying to talk Sam out of the way he felt he said, "we came here, Sam to drink some cold beers and watch this young lady dance, so why don't we get started doing it, right after we have some supper okay,!

The waitress came over and took their order for a big platter of tacos, beans and rice, and was instructed by Trudeau to bring them two beers apiece immediately. It seemed that Trudeau was serious about drinking some beer, so Sam thought to himself, "what the hell, I might as well join the party. "

The two men had just received their platter and their beers. When the runner for the telegraph office came into the cantina and it looked as if he had been running for a long distance. He seen Trudeau and Sam sitting at the table and ran over to them and headed Sam a telegram. Opening up the telegram Sam read it and then handed it to Trudeau.

It reads "Rangers post in Abilene attacked and destroyed by Klein's gang, stop, all prisoner's set free ,stop, Ranger Thompson killed, stop, your two deputies already on train headed home, stop, "it was sent by the town council of Abilene. The telegram ended "Klein gang believed to be headed your way, stop,"

There is one thing for sure, and two things for certain Klein and his gang is not going to be here tonight, so we have time to prepare for them, just in case they come this way. Trudeau said"

If we let them into town there is going to be a lot of innocent people get hurt, if there's any way we can. We need to catch them out of town, the only problem there is, and finding enough men willing to make up a posse large enough to take them on, Klein, by now has probably got 20 to 25 men riding with him. The only good thing is that he has to put out scouts, which will cut his numbers by at least 10 men and that could work in our favor, if we can catch these men and stop them from reporting back to Klein, then he would have to ride blind. That would give us a chance to set up an ambush. In my way of thinking that the only way we can even the odds."

Neither Sam nor Trudeau felt much like partying after receiving the telegram from Abilene, so they sat quietly drinking their beer and pondering what to do just in case Klein shows up in El Paso. If there was any troops anywhere close Trudeau could request them, but there wasn't and wouldn't be in the near future. This war between the States was taking its toll on the people of the South, but thank God it hadn't reached El Paso yet. This conflict between the North and the south was killing a lot of good men on both sides. Since it hadn't reached this far west by now, it probably wouldn't. It had been said that Klein started out fighting for the South, and then found out that it was easier to rob and kill innocent people, than it was to fight someone that could fight back.

Trudeau broke the silence, when he looked at Sam and Said, "if we only had some kind of idea where Klein and his bunch is, then we could possibly figure out what to do but the way things are we have no idea of where he's headed, only where he's been. I imagine that the Rangers has got all of their staff out looking for any kind of trail that will tell them at least what direction Klein is headed. I will tell you this, that if I get the chance I won't try to arrest him, but I will use a shotgun on him, and animal like him does not deserve to be hung and destroy a good rope."

The only way we're going to do something like that Trudeau is if somebody goes out and scouts back forward Abilene, there has to be a trail out there somewhere, and if they plan on holding up, they'll have to do it where there's water and the place must be isolated. The only place that I know that even remotely fits that scenario is a long, the red River, there are places along that river that you could hide an army. Maybe that's what Klein is counting on. If he doesn't show up in the next couple of weeks I think I might take a ride and scout out the red river area. One man just might be able to negotiate that river without drawing much notice."

Now, Sam, don't you go thinking that you're another version of Jim Bridger or Dahl Boone or even Davy Crockett. You're a law man that has sworn to uphold the laws of the Land and protect the people there in. If Klein comes this way then we'll deal with it, but until then, our responsibility is this town and the people in it."

I know Trudeau, but I joined the Rangers to stop people like the ones who murdered my family and Klein is one of those people, and I swore then I would even the score with anyone who took up that kind of life, and I will if it's the last thing I do."

The waitress came by the table to see if they needed any more beers before she started dancing, Trudeau, smiled real big and said, "yes, ma'am, we do, and I'd say you need to bring us at least three a piece, because once you get started dancing I doubt very seriously if we'll be able to get any more beer until you quit, " She smiled and danced away to the bar and within minutes she returned with three mugs in each hand, When she set the beers down the band started playing and it was as if someone had flipped as switch on her, because she started dancing and the minute she did everyone, including Sam and Trudeau started hollering. It wasn't long at all until the contents of that telegram was forgotten and the night was filled with laughter and a good time for all. It would have been an extremely good night. If Dusty and Manuel were here to enjoy the evening also.

Sam and Trudeau spent the rest of the evening, just leaning back and enjoying the festivities and the dancing. The band that was playing was exceptionally good, the only thing was every song they sang, they sang in Spanish. Sam tried to concentrate in the words and see if he could learn to interpret what they were saying when he looked up the front door and saw Ms. Salazar and her oldest daughter come in. The second that she seen Sam and Trudeau if they minded if they joined them. Sam didn't waste any time in saying, "no ma'am, we don't mind at all." Then jokingly, Sam looked at Ms. Salazar and ask, "are you sure that you're old enough for a beer? "Then Sam really got a surprise when she said, "I drink beer every once in a while, but tonight I am drinking tequila, and so is my daughter,"

Trudeau. Spoke up and said, "I am not going to sit here all night and call you Ms. Salazar, from now on you are Consuela and your daughter is Lolita, I hope that's all right with you. When Consuela and Lolita are such pretty names." Being a gentleman, Sam got up and pulled the chair out for Lolita and Trudeau pulled out a chair for Consuela. Trudeau got the other waitress attention and told her to bring them four shot glasses and a bottle of tequila. The waitress giggled and said, "It seems to me that you two gringos are ready to party." Then she looked at Sam and added, maybe you will dance with the señorita at least once tonight, especially after the tequila introduces itself to you,"

Lolita looked over at Sam and ask, "Why do you seem to be afraid to talk to me, I won't hurt you… much. " Consuela looked at Lolita and said, "shame on you, can't you see that you have embarrassed the Ranger, his face is a bright pink" and then she laughed, it was a good laugh, a true laugh, not a laugh that was put on in any way. Sam thought to himself, "it's been a long time since I have had a good night of fun, there are two beautiful ladies sharing our table. So, you big dummy. Let your hair down and enjoy the night"

Sam was really surprised when Consuela took Trudeau by the hand

and said, "come in gringo tonight, you do not sit, tonight you will dance every dance with me"

Lolita smiled at Sam and he knew there was no sense in arguing, so he took off his hat, took off his side arm and before Lolita could say anything, he took her by the hand and they hit the dance floor. For some reason everyone there started clapping and stomping their feet as the band played some kind Mexican song that called for a lot of stomping, so all Sam could do was to follow Lolita's lead.

After about 10 minutes, Sam told Lolita "I have got to sit down and get a drink of something can we take a break for a few minutes?" she looked at Sam , smiled and said, "I thought you would never ask, I am just a little bit out of breath myself." When Trudeau and Consuela seen Sam and Lolita sit down, they decided it was time for them to take a break also. Everyone sit down at the table, picked up a beer and a shot of tequila, toasted to each other. Then the two ladies licked salt off of their hand, downed the tequila, and took a bite out of a lime. Sam asked Lolita if that was the proper way to drink tequila. She smiled a very warm and playful smile and said, "My dear Sam, there is only one way to drink tequila and you just seen the right way."

Trudeau and Sam had danced the night away with these two beautiful ladies and in Sam's mind it was the most enjoyable evening that he had ever spent and he was already looking forward to the next time that he was fortunate enough to be allowed to spend the evening in their company, Finally, the waitress came over and said they would be closing in about 30minutes, So if they wanted one more drink they had best get it now. Both ladies decided they did not want another drink, so they finished off the beer and tequila that they had and got up to leave. When they walked out the door there was a buckboard tied to the hitching post. Consuela looked over at Trudeau and said, "I know where Sam is going, but can I give you a lift Marshall?"

"Trudeau was quick to answer "Consuela, I understand that you have an empty room at your boarding house, do you think it would be possible for me to occupy that room on a regular basis?"

"With you and Sam both staying in my boarding house there will be no reason why me or my family would ever feel as if were threatened by anyone, so yes Sir, I would be more than happy if you decided to move in to the room right next to Sam and become a permanent fixture in my humble house."

"Well then Miss Salazar I reckon that if you don't mind I will go home to my new room and I will move my belongings in tomorrow, if that's all right with you?" "It most certainly is Mr. Trudeau."

Consuela and Lolita got into the seat in the buckboard while Sam and Trudeau sat on the back. Consuela handled that buckboard like a professional and it was only a few minutes till they were at the boarding house. Consuela got down, and her daughter started to unhitched the team, well, that didn't sit right with Sam, so he hold the ladies to go inside, and he and Trudeau would take care of the team, besides it would give Sam and Trudeau, a chance to talk, and maybe smoke one last cigarette before hitting the hay.

Sam told Trudeau, "Sometime within the next three or four days I think I'm going to take a ride east and see what I can find out. By then Dusty and Manuel will be back and everything will get back to normal. I doubt very seriously if Dusty or Manuel knows what happened to Ranger Thompson and his prisoners. Knowing those two young men. I wouldn't doubt a bit, but what they will want to go looking for Mr. Klein and his bunch, but under no circumstances can they do that, they are not experienced enough to take on something like that. If you will Trudeau, I want you to keep them busy in town, and I don't want you to tell them where I have gone. I will tell you now that I plan on getting out there and scouting the red river basin to see if my hunch is right. I'm telling you, just in case I don't get back in a week or so you'll know where to come looking."

"Sam, you are honestly going to scout that bunch all by yourself, aren't you?" "I believe that one man traveling alone would have more of a chance of spotting them, then sending in a 25 or 30 man posse that could be seen for 10 miles by the Dust they leave behind. But anyway I won't leave for three or four days. That will give me more of chance of cutting their trail, if they're coming this way, which I believe they are. Tight now. Milliard, I am tired and sleepy and tomorrow morning is going to come awful early so what you say, let's call it a night,"

When the sun came up the next morning, Sam was already at the telegraph office and had sent a telegram to the Ranger station in.

Abilene, Texas, notifying them that he would be coming, and he would take over the investigation and the trailing of Klein and his gang, Sam's intention was to catch the next eastbound train, but he wanted to wait for Dusty and Manuel to return, this way he could make sure Dusty and Manuel did not take off on their own, seeking vengeance for Ranger Thompson. Just knowing that he had been murdered in cold blood would be enough.

Sam had waited for about an hour and a half to get a reply from Abilene, when it finally came his orders were quite clear. Find Alan Klein and bring him to Justice, or kill him. In order for Sam to do this, he needed a wanted dead or alive poster on Alan Klein alone, just to make it legal, after Sam received the telegram he headed back to Ms. Salazar's boarding house to gather up his bedroll and a couple of shirts and a couple pair of jeans along with long johns and some socks. And then will come the hard part, telling them that he was leaving town to lead the manhunt for the Klein gang, and letting them know that he wouldn't be back until the job was done. While he was at the telegraph office, he had sent another telegram to all telegraph stations all the way to Laredo to intercept Ben Johnson and ask him to return to El Paso to cover for him while he backtracked Alan Klein and his gang. The only thing Sam had left to do was talk to Dusty and Manuel and say goodbye to Trudeau.

Going back to his office after gathering up what he needed for the trip, he found Trudeau, sitting at his desk and going through wanted posters. He had one wanted poster laying out on the edge of the desk, so that it was in plain view. Picking up the wanted poster, Sam said "you must have been reading my mind Trudeau," it was a wanted dead or alive poster on Alan Choctaw Kline.

"I really wish that you would take two or three guys with you anyway," Sam turned and looked at Trudeau "I have a destiny to fulfill, Milliard, I Know what is waiting for me and I know that I must follow this trail, but even if this is the last time you see me, it will not be the last time that we will meet, if something happens to me just remember that anytime you feel a cold breeze across the back of your neck, or you think you hear somebody say something it will be me, no matter what. Milliard, I will always have your back, always believe that and remember what I have told you."

Without saying anything else, Sam Left the office carrying a Winchester and a shotgun and a half dozen boxes of ammunition. He walked slowly to the livery stable, saddled his horse and secured his bedroll and his saddlebags. He put the Winchester in the boot and tied the shotgun on top of his bedroll. He stepped up into the saddle, turned his horse south and at a slow walk. He headed toward the railway station.

As Trudeau watched Sam, he noted how tall in the saddle he sat, and the look of pride and determination on his face. It was at that instant, Trudeau knew that Sam would not be coming back, this would be his last trail and there was nothing that he could do about it, there was no way to change Sam's mind, he knew what he had to do and he would do it, no matter what.

Sam couldn't bring himself to look back, he wanted to remember the smiles and laughter from the people that he cared the most about. He wanted to remember their kindness, their understanding and their dedication to one another. In his dreams he had seen himself and the end, but he knew no matter what ever event produced his Downfall. It would be avenged by someone he had never met, and that someone would be wearing not the badge he has on now, but another badge, a broken badge.

There was a war between the North and South that had ended some years back, but the land and the people of the turmoil and pain that this war had caused. Klein was one of these pains, he had fought for the north and had been convicted of while in uniform, of robbing banks and killing people. He used to brag that he was the North's answer to Quantrill riders, but in fact he was just the leader of an outlaw gang that valued only money and produced death, pain and misery in any direction that they traveled.

He could hear the whistle of the westbound train, so Sam spurred his horse into a gallop, so he would be at the depot. When the train stopped. He had to have a heart-to-heart talk with Dusty and Manuel and explain to them that only part of the job that Sam didn't like, the part if relaying bad news was something that Sam did not like, and usually he would put that off on someone else, but not this time, this time it was left up to Sam.

As the train pulled into the depot, the first thing Sam seen was Dusty and Manuel, while he was still mounted on his horse the two young deputies walked up to Sam, their faces were beaming with the smiles that only young people can possess . Sam hated to do it, but he believed the best way to deliver bad news was just say it and get it out of way . So without a moment's hesitation, Sam said. "Fellers, I've got some bad news for you, after you left Abilene, Alan Klein and his gang perpetrated a jailbreak and in the process they killed ranger Thompson. I'm on my way there now to take over him. I'm going to be gone for quite a while, so I want you to learn up with Marshall Trudeau and Ben Johnson when he gets here, and protect this town. Manuel I left a letter laying on my bed, see that your mother gets it. "Sam heard a noise behind him, turned and there was Trudeau in a buckboard, smiling, he said, "I didn't think you two young fellers would mind ride back to town, but if you want to walk you can "!

"It feels so good to be back home, that I would crawl on my belly to get there, Dusty said" Manuel was already in the buckboard. He looked at Trudeau very seriously and said, "Let's go. Trudeau, there are things that I have to do, and we mustn't hold the ranger up, there are places he needs to go and things he must do,"

Off in the distance Sam could hear the whistle of the eastbound train, so he shook hands with the two young deputies, nodded at Trudeau and said, "Till the future, Trudeau and to a better time."

Sam then turned his horse and rode to the south side of the building, dismounted, and waited for the train to stop. The conductor let down the boarding ramp and took Sam's horse into the cattle car and secured him. Sam in the meantime had went in and signed a voucher for his train ticket to Abilene. As he boarded the train. The thing he seen was the buckboard headed north.

The long train trip to Abilene allowed Sam time to go back through the years and remembering all the things that it happened that were good for him, at the same time trying not to remember the bad things. He thanked God for the kindness of Ben Johnson and for all the things that he taught him. Been had taught Sam that dedication to a cause was an honorable thing, he also taught him that determination was a necessity, and that loyalty and honor were two things that you could not live without. He thought of his mother and father, his two brothers, and sister. Maybe when this trip over, he just might swing by Nacogdoches and see his sister. It had been almost 25 years since he had seen his sister and just maybe it's. Time to renew their family ties. He thought of all the things that he had done with Ben Johnson, of the outlaws that the two of them had tracked down, the people that they had helped, and the ones that they couldn't help.

There had been a peacefulness come over Sam, since he had started remembering all the things of his life and deep in his heart he knew that this trail would be his last, but he was disturbed about it. All of Sam's life he had been a believer in the hereafter, in Angeles, and in God, and in reincarnation. Sam had not made it a practice of reading in the Bible, but he taught tonight, he just might.

Sam did not know what was in store for him in Abilene, he only knew that he had to go and do his best to set things right for Ranger Thompson. There was no doubt in Sam's mind that his destiny had been preordained, the fact that this had all been set in motion, even before he was born made Sam believe in his heart that the beliefs he had held onto for so many years were coming true.

The rest of the trip to Abilene he spent reading his bible and talking to the other passengers. There was one young boy about the age of eight or nine who asked Sam a whole lot of questions, but his main question was how old you had to be before you could become a Ranger? As he watched the eyes of the boy's mother. Sam realized what he must tell to the young man, so Sam said. "There has been Rangers as young as 18, but my advice to you son is concentrate on just being an up standing citizen and honoring your mother and father. The life of a Ranger is a lonely life, the hours are long and so are the trail that you must ride. As long as your mother is on this earth you should resign yourself to making sure that she is taking care. Don't be in a hurry to become a Ranger. There will always be bad Man, and plenty of them. Go to school, get an education so you can get a job that is eight hours a day or even own your own buy, it will be up to you, so don't be in a hurry son to become a man,"

After Sam had talked to the young man. He could tell that the young man's mother was relieved by what Sam had told her son. When Sam asked about the boy's father. The lady told him that he had been killed during the war and that they were on their way to visit his grave, and to meet for the first time hid family who now lived in Norfolk, Virginia and had never seen their grandson, and if everything goes just right . Her and her son may stay in Norfolk, becoming the man that his father was.

CHAPTER 5

The next day when the train pulled into the depot in Abilene, the young man could not wait to say goodbye to his friend the Ranger, and it made Sam feel good that he had made a difference in the young man's life. He shook hands with Sam, just like a grown man would do and said with a big smile. "Save some bad guys for me one day when I'm older and bigger I will catch some of them too." "I believe you will son, Sam said. But for right now, you take care of your mama and listened to her, she won't teach you wrong."

Noticing that the conductor had his horse out of the cattle car, Sam said his goodbye's ad stepped off of the train, walked over to his horse, mounted him and sunk spur for downtown Abilene and the Rangers post. When he arrived at the post, he was surprised to find the state's attorney general sitting in the Rangers chair, also there was a judge, two council member and the country sheriff.

"Is there anything that I can do for you gentlemen? Sam asked" "we need to talk to you Ranger Cooper, I believe there has to some changes made in order to bring this gang of outlaws in and not give them a chance to get away," This statement came from the federal judge, and he continued, "you have been highly recommended by a lot of people some Texas Rangers and some are United States Marshall's, we have talked this over with the high officials in Austin, and they agreed that what we have in mind should be done. Mai I have your badge Ranger?" "What do you want with my badge? Sam asked" this time it was atty. Gen. That spoke "as of right now Cooper, you are no longer a Texas Ranger, let me explain why. To catch This band of outlaws you are doing to have to cross State lines and you can't do that wearing a Rangers badge, so with the blessings of your Superiors and the office of the atty. Gen. Of the great state of Texas you are hereby appointed the post of United States marshal," the judge stood up and said, "raise your right hand and put your left hand on this Bible, then repeat after me. I Samuel Cooper, do hereby swear to uphold all laws of the United States, so help me God."

After Sam had repeated what the judge said, the atty. Gen. Pinned a brand new united states Marshall's badge on his chest and said, "now son, there are no boundaries that can stop you from bringing this bunch of murderers to Justice, I change you Sir, with the responsibility of bringing this case and all responsible parties before the federal judge. Posted in Abilene, Texas. "

That's what I'm here to do, Sir, and I will not stop until I have completed my job. I don't have a whole lot of time to talk, I have an idea where these men have gone, but I can't swear to it. I've got to do some scouting on my own and find out for sure before I call for a posse. In this case the posse will have to be nothing short of a small army. The last time that I checked Alan Klein had somewhere in the neighborhood of 25 to 30 men riding for him, and they are all killers. So if you gentlemen will excuse me. I need to get to the hotel and get a good night's rest for an early start in the morning. Is there anyone here who can take my house to the stable? Tell the livery Nan to feed him good and rub him down, he's got a long way to go, and it's going to be a long time before he sees another town."

The next morning, Sam was up bright and early and had stopped in the hotel restaurant to have breakfast. When the sheriff walked in and when he motioned for him to sit down and said" you're up kind early aren't you sheriff?"

"Yes, I am Marshall, I wanted to see you before you took off and wish you luck in the world. I don't think I have to remind you that these people are sadistic cold-blooded killers, and it seems that they enjoying killing lawman the most so I urge you not to take any chances, if you find them get to the nearest place that you can get a posse and get one. You've got an awful big load on your shoulders, I wish I could take some of it off of you, but I can't," Then the sheriff looked over to the waitress and told her, "his breakfast is on the city of Abilene, just let him sign the ticket and we'll take care of it."

Then without saying anything else, just a nod of his head and a handshake, the sheriff turned and walked out the door and was gone. Sam thought ti himself, "this is probably the last time that you and I will ever meet."

After finishing his breakfast, Sam went to the livery stable and picked up his horse, then he went to the general store and picked up a slab of bacon, some coffee and sugar, beans, tobacco and rolling papers, and a small bag of flour, salt and pepper. He placed all of this in his saddlebags, along with his ammunition. Then he remounted his horse, took one last look at the town of Abilene, then he put his focus in the direction of the red river basin and started off at an easy gallop, the beginning of a long and dangerous journey.

It was going to take a good hard two day ride to get the red River and then the slow and tedious ride south into the badlands. He would have to take this time and be extremely vigilant and aware of his surroundings, one mistake would mean the end and this couldn't be over until he had done his job. Sam had decided that once he reached the red river he would travel by night and hold up during the day. This would make it easier for him to find Klein, because they would have a fire at night.

Every time that Sam would come close or pass by a ranch or a trading post, or a town, he would stop and inquire if anyone had seen a large number of men or seen a trail over which a large number of horses had ridden. The first day and half of the next day all the questions got no answers, but late in the afternoon of the second day, Sam didn't have to ask any questions he crossed the trail himself. Getting off if his horse. He studied the horse shoe prints and determine that there was between 20 and 30 men in this party, he could not be sure that it was Klein until he observed them, so he mounted back up and preceded to follow the trail. Just before midnight Sam seen campfires in up and preceded to follow the trail. Just before midnight Sam seen campfires in the distance. But then his enthusiasm vanished as he heard the mooing of a hard cattle. It was plain that the trail he had been following had been the trail of a cattle drive, probably headed to Fort Worth. He decided that he would ride on down and as some questions. Riding toward the sound of the cattle Sam was looking for and outrider to accompany him into the campsite just so he wouldn't get short by mistake, finally, in the darkness he seen the outrider and said in a voice very steady, strong, but not loud "this is US Marshall Sam Cooper, don't start shooting. I just need to get some answers to some questions, I need to talk to the trail boss I need you to take me into your camp."

There was no hesitation in the young cowboy he just motioned for his friend to come over and take his position and he said, "Come on Marshall I could stand a cup of coffee anyway." Sam followed the young wrangler into came and he was surprised to find half of the riders awake. Then the cowboy explained to him that they were working in shifts because they had come across a band of riders, and the way they looked at this heard the trail boss had got the idea they were thinking about trying to steal it, so they had doubled all night riders, and half of the wranglers were awake at all times.

The young cowboy poured Sam a cup of coffee and said, "sit down, relax Marshall I'll go wake up the ramrod of this here outfit, I won't be but a minute." As Sam sit there and his coffee, he noticed the wranglers were all well-armed and each man looked as if he would have no problem handling a gun. All of their side arms were hung low and tied down, if Sam didn't know better he would say that these men were on the wrong side of the law. But he had decided that these men were armed as they were to protect this herd.

The young cowboy returned and he was accompanied by a tall, muscular middle aged man with very distinguishing features and eyes that were cold and alert to any prospect of danger. He poured him a cup of coffee, sit down and looked at Sam. Then asked, "What can I do for you Marshall?

"I'm trailing a band of outlaws of outlaws who killed a Texas Ranger, then freed his prisoners and burnt his post to the ground. I understand from this young man that you have met a gang of men riding hard. What I need to know is you can remember, how many men?"

I can't remember exactly where we meet them, but I can tell you that their headed in the same direction we are"! "I kind of took for granted that you were headed for Fort Worth," "No sir, were headed for San Antonio. These cattle are not going to the slaughter house. They have been bought by a gentleman starting up a large cattle ranch south of San Antonio and about halfway to Laredo"

I've got the feeling, Sam said, that this bunch of men is headed for the lower end of the red river basin. They have to hide for a while to let things cool down after killing that Ranger, so I can't think of a better place to hide. The lower end of the red river basin is not fit for much of nothing and very sparsely populated."

"Why don't you ride along with us Marshall, we're all headed in the same direction and your company would be greatly appreciated, besides if it comes to it, me and the boys could give you whatever back up you need. This bunch is not afraid of a fight, every man here fought in the war between the States with the exception of my sin here." "I'm sorry paw that I wasn't born a few years earlier, the young wrangler said. "

Maybe I shouldn't say anything, it's really not my place, but young man be glad that you were born early enough that you didn't have to fought in that war. There is not a man a live who fought in that war who didn't lose almost everything he owned. A lot of good men on both sides died fighting for what they believed in. It was a hard and bloody time and a lot of mothers are still crying, a lot of children are growing up without their fathers, and a lot of Windows are living hard lives just trying to survive."

"Thanks for the invitation, Sam said, the more I think about it, the more I think it's good idea for me to ride along with you for a spell, just in case that bunch decides to double back, they won't catch me out in the open. But to be on the safe side. I'm going to put my vest back on to cover up this badge," "why don't you just take it off and put it in your pocket? The trail boss asked.

"I made a promise to the man who penned this badge on me that the only way it would ever come off would be if I was dead and I meant it," "I can't keep calling you trail boss, so what is your bane please?"

"My name is William Kilpatrick, but my friends call me Bill," "My name is Sam, and everybody calls me Sam Cooper, either one is fine with me. Personally I really don't like being called Marshall. Said in the wrong place at the wrong Time, it could out a target on my back, so please either Sam or Cooper is fine."

Bill looked at Sam and said, "If you care to put down your bedroll and get a few hours' sleep you're welcome. Whiskers, that's the Chuck wagon cook, he'll be starting breakfast in a couple of hours and then an hour after that, we'll start driving for the day, and you can ride along with me Sam if you want to?

"If I'm going to ride with this trail drive I need to be doing a job, and I know that the job most hated is trailing the heard, so that's the job I'll take, I'll eat the dust, so one of the other guys doesn't have to, if it's okay with you?"

Sam led his horse over to the picket line, unsaddled him and laid his saddle on the ground, then unrolled his bedroll, so that his head would be laying in the seat if the saddle. Removing his boots and his gun belt, Sam lay down and was asleep in no time.

It was almost like he had just closed his eyes when there came a sharp kick on the bottom if his foot to wake him up, the wrangler that was standing there, smiled and said, better get up and get your breakfast before someone else does."

It had been a long time but Sam remembered how life was on a trail drive and of how each member of that trail drive depended on the man next to him, not only for communications, or company, but for safety and companionship. A lot of friendship are made on trail drives and these friendship seem to last for the life of the two men that from this bond.

From the smell of breakfast they were having steak and eggs and a lot if coffee. Which suited Sam to a T. There was nothing that Sam like better than a steak cooked over an open fire, over medium eggs, and an endless cup of coffee.

This bunch of wranglers were well mannered, there was no pushing and shoving or jousting for position in the chow line. Each man stood in line and waited his turn to be handed a plate with three eggs and a steak with two biscuits on the side and a cup of coffee. There was no talking while they were eating each man know the day would bring and was preparing himself for the long, dusty day.

As Sam ate his breakfast he noticed each and every wrangler had his own set precedes of preparing for the day's drive. The one thing that Sam noticed was that each and every man made sure is riffle and his side arm was fully loaded and ready to go. It seemed that these cowboys were expecting some kind of trouble, so, following their lead. He made sure his Winchester was fully loaded and his shotgun, then he emptied his 45, cleaned it, reloaded it, making sure it was loaded all the way around. It was then that bills son walked over and sit down and asked, Sam "this band of fellers that you're chasing they did something really bad?" "Yeah, they murdered a Texas Ranger" Sam answered.

Without asking any more questions, the young wrangler got to his feet and preceded to saddle his horse, so Sam preceded to do the same. All of a sudden whiskers gave out a holler "I've got coffee left anybody want some before I pour it out?" Deciding that one more cup wouldn't hurt Sam headed for the Chuck wagon. The coffee was just the right temperature where you could turn it up and down it without scalding your tongue. Downing the coffee Sam handed the cup back to whiskers and said, "Thanks, that last cup sure did hit the spot." With a smile on his face and a nod of his head whiskers said, glad to have you aboard Sam, if you need anything, all you got to do is ask."

Whiskers, was a beanpole of a man, soaking wet he might weigh a hundred and 50 pounds, but the man could make a meal out of nothing and it would taste good. None of the cowboys gave whiskers any kind of trouble over his cooking, not even an occasional joke. I guess they knew that whiskers took his job very seriously, so they just left him alone.

The morning went by fast. These cowboys knew how to drive a herd of cattle and not run their fat off, they just keep them moving at an easy pace and making sure that no strays stayed behind. It was coming on to noon when Sam noticed that whiskers had pulled the Chuck wagon off to the side and each wrangler while staying on his horse went by and picked up a sandwich to eat while staying in the saddle. Deciding that he could use something too, Sam rode easy over to the chuck wagon, whiskers just looked up and smiled and handed Sam a roast beef sandwich on sour dough bread and it must have been 3inches thick, bread and all. Sam then done like all the other wranglers. Nodded his head, thanks and rode back to his position.

The rest of the day was just like the early ride of the morning, there was no hurry and each wrangler stayed in his post, and the cattle were quite content to keep moving without even trying to break ranks.

The sun was starting to set when the lead wranglers started the herd turning in a circle. It didn't take Sam long to understand why at the lead there was a large spring, which made this a perfect place to shut down for the night.

Whiskers had already stopped his wagon and unhitched his mules and was busy building a fire to start cooking. Bill came by and asked, Sam if he would mind taking the early sleep before they went and relieve him. Sam without any hesitation said that he would be more than glad to help out any way he could, besides Sam wanted some time alone to do some thinking and plan out what he was going to do when he met up with Klein and his gang. He just had a funny feeling that it wasn't going to be all that long before they met.

Sam figured that the red river basin was only about a two day ride ahead and that would be where he said goodbye to his newfound friends, and started downstream at a slow, steady pace traveling only by night . That was the easy part, the hard part would be making sure that this was Klein and his gang and not another cattle drive.

The night was peaceful and off in the distance Sam could hear one of the nighthawk riders singing a song. Most all of the cattle were bedded down and asleep, a few still stood, but before long, they too would call it a night. The moon was up and so bright that it was almost like daylight and the stars had never seemed as bright as they were tonight, there was a peaceful, almost spellbinding feeling that came over Sam and something in the back of his mind told him that it wouldn't be long before his destiny would be fulfilled and his spirit would be set free.

It had been almost 2 weeks since Sam had left El Paso and he wondered what Trudeau and the two deputies Dusty and Manuel were doing, and he thought about Ms. Salazar and her daughter, Lolita. He wondered if any of them ever thought about him, it was a stupid thought because he believed in his heart that they did worry about him and they were waiting for some kind of word from him, soon he would send a message if he could.

Off in the distance Sam could see another rider walking his horse slowly, so that he would not startle the cattle and start a stampede. Keeping an eye on the rider. Sam stayed alert until he recognized that it was bills son, and he was coming to relieve him. The young wrangler set the saddle as if he had been born into it, and there was a pride that shown in the way he rode his horse. Not many sons got to spend time with her father's after the war was over, a lot of the fathers never returned and the bad thing about it was that nobody really knew if they were alive or dead. A lot of the prisoners on both sides never made it out of places like Andersonville in the south, and of course the North had their version too. Sam had been lucky being with Ben Johnson had kept him out of the war or else he would have been one of the younger men who were usually the first to die, or all the very least lose an arm or a leg or be blinded.

"I take it that everything is quiet and peaceful." The young man said in almost a whisper. "It's so quite out here. I'm almost afraid to move. I'm afraid I'll disturbed something." Sam said as he turned his horse at a slow walk away from the herd and toward the campsite.

When he arrived at the campsite, it was the same as the night before, half of the cowboys were sleep, and half were preparing for their shift of being a nighthawk. The trail boss, Bill was still up and having a cup of coffee, when he seen Sam, he said, "picket your house and pull your saddle and bedroll and then join me for a cup of coffee." When he had finished with his horse Sam returned to the camp fire and sat down. Bill then handed Sam a cup of coffee and said, "tomorrow morning, Sam, we are going to turn the herd southeast, I sent one of my riders out ahead to see which direction that bunch was traveling, he came back and said that they kept a straight line and where we turn to go southeast they are going due east, I just figured you would want to know. "As soon as I finish this coffee. I'm going to lay down and get some sleep, I figure you'll probably be gone by the time I wake up, and so I'll say my goodbyes now." Sam said.

Sam finished his coffee and started over to his bedroll. When whiskers walked over to him and stuck out his hand and said, I'll say my goodbyes now son, won't have time in the morning, but I promise you this, I'll leave you a steak and biscuits and a pot of coffee next to the fire. You just remember to put the fire out before you leave, and I know you don't like to be called this but I'm going to say it anyway, it's been a pleasure knowing you Marshall and may God protect you. The old man then turned and walked away and it was as if his shoulders were carrying a heavy load. They seem to sag just a little from the weight of having to say goodbye, it was funny in a sense, because Sam felt the same weight on his shoulders. He had grown to like this bunch of men who done their job and minded their own business but were at the drop of a hat ready to stand up for friend, this bunch would be hard to forget.

Before Sam laid down he took a walk out into the night. He felt as if he needed to say a prayer and maybe have a talk with the lord about what the next few days were going to bring, but most of all it was to ask forgiveness, as he did every night, for things that he done, even in the line of duty that he felt he needed forgiveness for, he felt he even needed forgiveness for some of the thoughts that he had about Lolita and for some of the dreams that he had about her.

He seemed to feel more at ease after he had this evening talk, and it always helped him sleep. Sometimes Sam felt like his belief in the hereafter and in god, Angels, reincarnation, and of course the devil was just a way of making sure that his conscience were clear. As Sam stretched out in his bed roll once again, he looked around at the wranglers and wondered how many of them, if ask, would go with him, he was quite sure that if ask, only a skeleton crew would be left to attend the cattle, the rest would ride with him, but Sam put that thought out if his mind, because this was one ride that he had to take by himself. After he found the Klein gang, then he could find a posse and confront them.

Sam leaned back and laid his head on his saddle and while looking up at the sky, he wondered just what tomorrow would bring , and then he dozed off and began having dreams of people that he had met and of the things he had done. Then there were the sweet dreams that he had almost every night of sweet Lolita, Sam always felt that he would be smart to ask this girl for her hand, but Sam believing that he was going to die young. He didn't want to leave her a young widow with a child or two. Although he was quite sure that with her mother's help, she would survive and live a good life.

Sam was awakened by the movement in camp of the riders saddling up, as he sat up he could see the sun starting to rise in the east and he noticed the campfire was still going. Although the chuck wagon was already gone. There was a plate, and a pot of coffee and one cup sitting beside the fire, just as whiskers said there would be. Sam got up and slipped his boots on and walked over to the campfire, picked up the plate started eating, the. He looked up the sky, smiled and said, "Thanks, for another day and watch over me as my journey ends, and I pray you welcomed me with open arms.

By the time Sam finished his breakfast all of the wranglers had said their goodbyes and had moved off to the herd and had taken up their positions and started moving the cattle Southeast, Sam sat and watched them until they were out of sight, then he saddled his horse, lied down his bedroll, and the last thing he done was put out the fire. He then stepped into the saddle and headed out following the trail due east.

That Klein bunch was not trying to hide their trail instead the trail was not so clear that Sam could follow it at a gallop. He realized that they were leaving a trail, hoping that someone would follow it just so they could set up an ambush, after all, they had picked the way that they wanted to live, robbing and killing was a way of life now and there was no backing out of it. Sam rode till about 3 o'clock in the afternoon, then he made camp, so he could sleep for six or seven hours and then travel at night, hoping to catch sight of their campfires

The first night there was no campfires or anything else with the exception of the trail to say that this outlaw gang was anywhere in the vicinity come daylight San had found a groove of cottonwoods next to a spring so he made camp and settle down to get a long days sleep.

He must have been a lot more tired than he thought, because when he woke up, it was only about an hour to an hour and half until the sun was going to set. He then built a small fire, so he could fix a pot of coffee and some bacon and beans, as he was fixing his supper, he was thinking of the wranglers and wondering how far they had gotten and how they were doing some way he needed to get whiskers coffee pot back to him, he thought of Trudeau, the deputies, Mrs. Salazar and Lolita, he wondered if Ben Johnson had made it back to El Paso yet, or if he had even gotten the message that he had sent

For the first time in his life since his parents died, Sam felt alone, but riding at night was going to give him a chance to get a lot of stuff off of his chest and make peace with his maker. After eating Sam cleaned up, put out the fire, saddled his horse and started out riding east.

It wasn't long after dark till Sam seen a glow in the night sky. It was too bright to be a campfire, so, he spurred his horse into a gallop and in no time at all, he came upon a small ranch, that was on fire and a man, woman and two children lay dead in the front yard. They had been executed, shot to death. There were no weapons present, so they had been murdered in cold blood and left for the coyotes, wolves and buzzards to pick their bones clean dismounting Sam looked around and found a shovel and started digging. He dug one big grave, and finding a blanket that had not burned. He placed it over the bodies and preceded to cover them up. Not knowing the family's name. He made a wooden cross and took his pocket knife and carved into the crossed. "Here lies a family, man, woman, children, murdered, then he dated it 1879.

With the ranch still burning, Sam knew that the Klein bunch couldn't be far ahead. So he looked around and any stock, horses or cattle or pigs he released so they can fend for themselves until some other rancher came by and gathered them up.

Anger rose up inside of Sam as he climbed back in the saddle and went back to following their trial.

The rest of the night did not produce any campfires or any other

Sign of the gang, so the next morning, Sam found another ideal place to camp and set about building him a fire to brew some coffee and fix him some biscuits and fry some bacon. He was busy doing this when he heard a horse riding up, he reached and got this Winchester and stepped back among the cottonwoods, Sam watched as the rider got closer and then smiled in relief as bills son and two of the other wranglers rode up,

"Paw finally decided that it was wrong to let you ride off alone, so he sent us to ride with you and he said that we should not take no for an answer." Well. If you're going to ride with me ,at least tell me your names," Sam said as he was motioning for them to get down and have some coffee" I'm Pete Kilpatrick, this is shortly turn bull, and the other one is Stanley graves, we just call him , tombstone."

"Might as well make yourself comfortable, because the way I'm talking these man is at night. It seems to be safer that way and sooner or later they're going to have stop and make camp. That's when I'll see their campfires. I figure you all been riding most of the night anyway, so unsaddled your horse, gentlemen and put out your bedrolls cause I'm going to catch me a good long nap, I suggest you do the same."

The three wranglers set about unsaddling their horse and hobbling them so that they couldn't run off, but could still graze and get to the spring to drink. No one spoke. While they were laying out their bedrolls, they only started to speak when they broke out their own eats from their saddlebags and poured them a cup of coffee, it was then that Pete turned to Sam and said, "whiskers sent you something " He then handed Sam a fried dried apple pie Sam, smiled and poured him another cup of coffee, said thanks and then joined in the conversation, for the next hour or so they talked about any and everything Sam learned that their home ranch was just west of Weatherford, Texas, and that their nearest neighbor was a good 30 miles away. Pete said that he has brothers younger than him, plus four sisters. There was a full crew of wranglers still at the ranch keeping an eye on everything. So there was no need to worry about his mom or his brothers and sisters.

After a while the wranglers started yawning and then everyone decided it was time to lay down and sleep as everyone settle down, Sam said a silent prayer that the lord keep these young men safe and protect them, because they really had no idea what kind of a bunch of men they were going to encounter, knowing that these young men had never known men like this, Mr. Kilpatrick had done an excellent job of raising his son and if his son was anything like the rest of the family. Then he had a family that he could be extremely proud of, one of the wranglers picked a cup of coffee pot and poured it on the fire to put it out. Then got a full of water, shook it and poured it out. Getting rid of all the coffee grounds then he reached and got another pot of water and sat it where the fire was so they could have coffee when they woke up.

It took quite a while for the wranglers to get to sleep, simply because it's hard to sleep when you're usually working and work when you're usually sleeping everything gets turned around as if you were going backwards, but there was no way out, this is the way it had to be for safety sake.

Sam did not go to sleep right away, instead he wondered if he was doing the right thing by allowing these young men to ride with him. They were young, and full of fight, and as far Pete he would not disappoint his father in any way shape form or fashion. His father sent him to help. And help is what he going to do .Sam decided when he woke up he was going to test these young men and see just how good they were with their side arms, and with a rifle. So Sam said his silent prayer, and for the first time he asked his maker to keep him safe. He had thought a lot about Lolita and he felt that he now had a reason to want to live and he decided when this was all over and if he was still alive, he was going to asked Lolita to marry him.

When Sam woke up the sun was still high in the western sky, so he continued to lay there and relax. Being that all three of the wranglers were still asleep and there was no urgency in waking them up until the sun started going down, then he and the three wranglers would sit down and figure out a plan that they could use when they were going to be outnumbered at least 7 to 1, so these young men had best know how to shoot.

It wasn't long after Sam woke up till Pete stirred and when he was fully awake he woke the other two up. The first thing that shorty done was to start building a fire and making a pot of coffee, tombstone pulled out a slab of bacon and begin slicing it, by the time he had finished his work, there were four huge slaves of bacon per person. Pete had put on some beans to start cooking so Sam started making biscuits, together, the four of them made a pretty good team, at least in cooking, Sam would soon find out they could shoot, when everything was set on the fire to cook. Sam stood up and said, "Gentlemen, hate to do this but I need to know just how good you are with your weapons" Pete stood up and pointed out a lamb on a tree about 50 yards away. He lined the other two up beside him and told them to fire in sequence, he would hit the lamb first, then shortly would hit the lamb second and tombstone would hit it last each man fired once, Pete took the end of the lamb off, shorty shot the lamb in half, and when tombstone shot, there was no lamb left." All Sam could think to say was well, I don't guess I have to worry about if you can shoot anymore," "Knowing how to use a weapon, and knowing when to use weapon, is something that my father is very stem about, he is a firm believer that every man that works for him, paw started teaching me to use a weapon when I was old enough to carry one, "Pete said, and in agreement. The other two wranglers shook their heads and said that Mr. Kilpatrick had also taught them how to use weapon and they added that the reasons Mr. Kilpatrick sent the three of them was because he considered Pete, shortly, and tombstone the best he had, and he wanted Sam to have all the help that he could possibly get.

All four men, then settled back and tended to their cooking, it was the that the youngness in these three wranglers showed up as they started telling stories about their adventures while working for Mr. Kilpatrick and laughing at their mistakes that they made, and how scatterbrained they was when they first hired on, then they would praise Mr. Kilpatrick for having the strength to put up with young men so full of vinegar that they didn't know which direction they wanted to go. They all agreed that there were days when he had to start them in the right direction and then watched them to make sure they stayed in that direction. It was fun to Sam, just to listen to them talk as if they were a lot older wranglers were 21 years old, it was a miracle.

Their supper was finally ready and the four men sat down to eat their bacon, beans and biscuits. Sam told shorty that he made the best coffee he'd ever tasted, but he was not to tell whiskers that Sam said so.

After they had finished their meal Sam decided that it might not be a bad idea to start out a little earlier than usual, that way they could travel a little faster until it got dark. Then they would have to slow down to walk and keep their eyes peeled for any signs of a campfires, and he fold the young wranglers to keep sniffing the air to see if they smelled smoke. If these men were accustomed to the trail they would use dead Mesquite to build their fire. Simply because dead mesquite does not smoke, but it does put out a lot of heat. To keep the young men from talking too much, Sam told them to stretch out, keeping at least 20 feet between each man and stay in line.

Once they had formed a pan everyone saddle their horse, while cleaning up the campsite shorty noticed that there was alone rider on the ridge, about 300 yards away, watching them, Sam told all the three men to act as if they had not seen the stranger and carry on with their business of breaking camp, after dark they would set a trap for the rider, so they could find out why he was watching them Sam would know if it was one of the Klein's men by the shape that his horse was in.

Acting as if there were in no hurry they mounted their horses and started walking as if they were searching for stray cattle. Which in this area people would do because there was a lot of wild long horns that roamed free and instead of buying cattle a lot of new ranches would gather these longhorns up and tame them. Then breed them and start their herds that way. Seeing ranch young wranglers knew this and they knew how they had to act so they split up each man going in different direction, searching for any sign of these cattle. While searching each man made sure that he was in sight of one other man, that way everyone would know where everyone else was. And that was very little chance of being ambushed.

The make believe search for cattle carried on right up until the sun went down, then all four men took off in four different direction with their destination being the last place that they see the stranger, circling around the area, the four men started closing in and leaving no way for the stranger to get away, the stranger was busy watching the nearest rider in front of him and didn't see the other three and they were on him before he could react. When Pete told the man raise his hands, the man turned around and it was the prisoner, that dusty and Manuel had transported to Abilene. When he seen Sam, he went for his gun and Pete pulled his trigger and lane died before he hit the ground.

"I wish he hadn't gone for his gun, I don't know if we could have gotten anything out of him, but I would've sure love to have tried," Sam said. Pete put his gun back in his holster and said," I'm sorry Sam, but when he went for his gun, I just reached the way paw taught me"

"Well, there's one thing for sure Klein and his bunch can't be too far away, they've got to be pretty close so that his outriders could report to him, now all we have to do is, find him, has anybody got a shovel? If not, let's gather up some rocks and bury him above ground. Somebody take his gun belt and anything else in his pockets, shorty you check out his saddlebags, tombstone you unsaddled his horse take the bridal off of it and turn it loose."

It took a little while to find enough rocks to cover Lane above ground, after they had finished stacking the rocks Sam turned to the three wranglers and said, " now more than ever fellas, we have to be quite and move slow, I want you to spread out and form a picket line where everyone is about 200 feet apart, remember move slow and quite, you see or smell anything get to the person nearest you and tell him , he in turn will tell the next person and so on, until we can all gather in the same place" agreed?

These young men were quite exceptional they had been taught to follow orders and not to stray from them, and they had learned their lessons well, streaming out into a picket line where everyone could see everyone else, they started moving forward slowly and quietly and each man had his Winchester in his hand and ready to use it if necessary.

The only real chance that these four men had was complete surprise. They all knew this, but yet the young wrangler's never balked and never questioned anything, Sam said these were the kind of men that would stand beside you, no matter what the odds.

The picket line carried on until the sun starting to rise, it was then that tombstone, waved his arms and pointed, the other three men moved to him quickly to see what he was pointing at. Off in the distance you could see a pale cloud that looked like a smoke so quietly the four men walked their horses to the base of the next hill then dismount did and walked up to the top and lay down on their belly's. There were no horses, and no men. But they had been there because their fires were still burning. Tombstone looked at Sam and ask, "Do you want me to ride down there acting like a cow hand, that's worried about them fire?" "Are you really that good on actor tombstone? Sam asked "yes, sir. Believe so, I have fooled a few people in my life, shouldn't be any problem"

Sam nodded his head" yeah go ahead and we'll do our best to cover you from here when you get there make the appearance that the fires are the only thing that you're worried about, go straight for them, and start putting them out okay?

Tombstone went back down the hill hopped on his horse and headed for the campsite, when he got to the campsite he stayed on his horse for just a minute. Turning his horse in a circle and looking as if he was trying to see who the fires belong to, seeing no one, he dismount it and preceded to put out the campfires. He got all the fires put out and then knelt down looking at the tracks and pointed due South

CHAPTER 6

Sam and the two remaining wranglers made their way down to the campsite very cautiously, when they had met up with tombstone he told them that the tracks said that they had split and gone in six different directions and to the best his ability, he would say that there were four horses in each party, but there was only one party that headed West, The rest had gone either due South, due East and one had gone Northeast .Tombstone said, "If I had to pick which one was Klein, I would say the party that headed West, if things are hot enough for Klein to run, then the best place to run, is the New Mexico territory once he's there, he can go any direction, on to Arizona, or south to Mexico, north to Colorado, or even further West to California."

Listening to the young wrangler, Sam found himself agreeing with him and said, you say there is only four in the party going west? That means that Klein has made arrangement with the rest of his gang to lay out false trails and then meet back with him at a certain spot. My way of thinking is that he is headed directly for the place they are to meet because he wants to be safe. He's it coward without his gang to back him up."

Then smith turned and locked ate Pete, Shorty, and tombstone and said, "You have not only made your dad proud, but you have ridden with pride for the brand. I really do appreciate everything you've done so far, but as of now it is my job to go after the one you believe is Klein I suggest that you three rejoin Mr. Kilpatrick on his trail drive, what has to be done now only I can do there's no need for you to put yourself in danger, it's time for me to do my job."

With that Sam, mounted his horse found the trail heading due west and took off a t a gallop. Meanwhile, the three young wranglers sat and watched Sam disappear from sight, Pete then said "Whoever that man's father is. He should be mighty proud of that menthe's one of a kind."

Mounting their horses, the three young men turned their horse Northeast, Pete figured they would be moving slowly Southeast coming in a direct line to meet them.

Turning to take one last look in the direction that Sam was last seen the trio spurred tier horses into a gallop in anticipation of meeting up with the herd and the boss. It just might be possible for them to meet before the dark, but it mean a hard day's ride

The trial was easily followed, they didn't seem to be in any hurry evidently they thought that no one would be trailing them, but they were wrong there was death of ranger Thompson that had to be avenged.

They had found the complete on the east side of the red River, so, that meant they had to cross over it again going west. There were only a couple of places that was suitable to fording the river, it would seem that they would need to camp and rest their horses, and what better place than in the grasslands on the west side of red River. When Sam had been with ben Johnson they had traveled this area quite often and he remembered both pieces to, because the trail was leading directly at them, so Sam, spurred his horse on, hoping to catch up with these four just about dark. If he could, it would give him the advantage of

Surprise that he so desperately needed. He knew he could not stand face to face against all four men in daylight, to try to do so would be deadly.

On thought the day and into late evening Sam made good time following the trail. Then about an hour or so before sunset. Sam seen smoke in the distance, not enough for it to be a building, but enough for a good campfire. Slowing down to a walk. Sam made his way very cautiously to a ridge overclocking where the smoke seemed to be coming from as he crawled on his belly up to the top of the ridge. He looked down and he recognized two of the men at the campfire, they were two of the men that he and Trudeau had kicked out of El Paso. When they had kicked. Wells out of the town for running a crooked gambling house and saloon,

Sam was fully convinced now that these four men were headed

back to El Paso for some reason or another. Maybe his best bet would be to trail them for a while and see that they were up to. This meant that Sam would have to run a cold camp, there would be no coffee and he would have to eat beef jerky and cold biscuits. He needed to be far enough away so that if this horse made any noise these men wouldn't hear him, but he still needed to be where he could see these men, So, Sam figured he would wait until dark. Then he would move around to a point where he could still see their fire, but they couldn't see him or his horse.

Just as the sun was going down Pete and his two friends sited the herd, they had already been bedded down for the night, and he could see the Chuck wagon and one large campfire, Pete was anxious to get back to doing his job as a ranch hand, but he still wondered about Sam and how he was doing. He knew that his father would be disappointed that they didn't stick with him, but they had been taught to follow orders and Sam was a marshal and had told them to leave, his father would understand, he wouldn't like it, but he would understand it.

When they rode into camp Mr. Kilpatrick was the first one to meet them, he greeted his son with a handshake and a hug, then a handshake and a hug for the both shortly and tombstone. After finding out that they were all okay. He then asked about Sam "Did the Marshall get his men? Or he still chasing them?"

"It's down to four men paw and he told us that the rest was up to him and that we should come back and rejoin the drive. He thanked us for our help, but there was no sense in us putting our lives in danger anymore. It was time for him to do his job, we didn't want to leave him, but he insisted, he also said that you would understand why he had to do this alone?"

"I almost certainly do don, a mass's duty to his job means everything to a man like Sam, and his very existence depends on loyalty, determination and pride."

When the whiskers found out that the three wranglers were back the first thing he asked was "did you give Sam the fried dried apple pie? What did he have to say about it? Is he okay? Well, how about it will one of you please answer my questions?"

"We trailed the gang and they split up, so with tombstones help

Sam decided to follow one group that he was pretty sure Klein was part of. The others headed off in at least three different directions. The last time we saw Sam, he was headed do west following at the trail of the four men that he thought were leaders of the gang, and they were headed as straight as you could go for El Paso. You do know whiskers, That El Paso is where Sam stationed. He was a ranger in El Paso, but when he went to Abilene, The Texas Atty. Gen. and a federal judge talked to his bosses in Austin and in order for him to chase this bunch he needed to be capable of crossing state lines and pursuing them in territories and the only way he could do that was to become a US Marshall"

Mr. Kilpatrick broke into the conversation and said, "I still don't like the idea of the Marshall chasing those men by himself, So Pete as soon as you rest and getting something to eat. I want you to saddle a fresh horse, and there's a railroad crossing about 20 miles behind us, there is also a water tower, I want you to go there and when the train stops to take on water, I want you to have them send a telegram to the US Marshall's office in El Paso telling them where Sam is, and requesting that they send him help. Make sure that you give them any information that Sam left with you. Such as did he say anything about where he thought these men were going? If he did make sure that you write it down and get it sent as soon as possible, tell the engineer that he is in danger and he needs help.............immediately!"

" Oh by the way whiskers, Pete said, Sam liked the fried dried apple pie, but he made me promise not to tell you that he did, he said you head was big enough already, because you knew you could cook."

"You just wait till I see him again, I'll teach him to tell people I've got a big head," whiskers was still mumbling to himself when he turned and walked back toward the Chuck wagon, But Pete could tell that the old man was pleased as punch that Sam liked his fried dried apple pie, Sam had made a big impression on whiskers just by the way that he treated him. Sam always answered yes, Sir and no, sir, and he never forgot to say please and thank you

The sun had gone down and Sam had started circling the campsite to get in a good position to keep an eye on them so that they couldn't pull out without him knowing it. he found the ideal place and hobbled his horse , then settled down to watch, he figured that they would break camp long before daylight and move out in as straight of a line as they could.

Sam must have dozed off for just a few minutes because he was awakened by the judge of a Winchester in his back. Startled Sam started to stand up, that's when he was hit in the back of the head. The next thing he knew, he and his horse were in the camp and he was tied to a Cottonwood. When he started to stir the four men stood up and walked over to him and one man said, "Look, the sleeping beauty has woke up, looks like we've captured us a US Marshall."

"Unite me and I'll show you who's been captured Sam said" I guess it upset the tail man, he drawback and kicked Sam in the stomach and then hit him with fist on his left cheek bone cutting it .Sam could feel the blood running down his cheek and he swore to himself.

The four men preceded to go back to the campfire laughing and sat down, the tall man that had just hit him said," I'll bet you my share of the next bank we hit, that I can hit his badge from here. The other three men all said, "Klein you're not a good shot, I for one will take that bet. " Sam said, "So, you're Alan Klein, I buried the man and woman and their kids that you killed at that little ranch, about three days back. Why did you kill them Klein? The man or the woman either one was not armed and dim quite sure the kids weren't armed either."

"The man would not swap us fresh horses, we even tried to buy them, but he just would not sell or trade" Klein stated with a cockeyed smile on his face."

"I guess it makes you feel awful big to kill women and children, doesn't it? The minute, Sam said that he knew he had made a mistake because Klein's face turned while and without any hesitation at all, he drew his 45 and fired. Sam felt the bullet go deep into his shoulder just to the left of his badge, the one of the men laughed and said "Well, it looks like we get your share Klein, because you missed that badge a good 3 inches." Klein stood up, his face still white with anger and said," Do you have anything else to say marshal before you die."

"Kill me if you must, but remember what I tell you I curse you. Alan Choctaw Klein. There will be another who will take my place and he will bring you down, this cursed I placed on you. And when this man comes for you. He will be in his right hand.

That's when Klein completely lost it, he took four or five steps getting closer to Sam, and he leveled his 45 and fired almost point blank at Sam's badge. The force of the bullet hitting his chest knocked the breath out of Sam and he could see the blood running freely down his shirt front, he knew then this would be his last day. Slowly, as Sam sat on the ground still tied to the three. He watched the life run down to his chest, and he knew he was going to die right here in this lonely little place on the banks of the red River. The last thought that came to Sam's mind was Lolita, and then he was gone.

It was the next day in El Paso, When the young runner from the telegraph office came into Trudeau's office at a dead run carrying a telegram, without pausing, he handed the telegram to Trudeau and went back out the door, Trudeau opened up the telegram and started reading, all of a sudden he sat up straight and told the two deputies to get all three men's horses saddled up stocked up with ammunition and food and be ready ride in an hour. He then handed the telegram to dusty, he read the telegram and handed it to Manuel, after the two men had read the telegram. Without saying a word, they left the Marshall's office with a grim look on their face and tears in their eyes.

Mr. Kilpatrick could not stand the fact that Sam was out there chasing these outlaws alone, so he gathered his men around and told them, "There is a Marshall out there somewhere chasing down some cold-blooded killers. And he's doing it by himself. We only have about 20 miles to go, so, I am leaving only enough men to finish this drive everyone else will come with me Pete, shorty, tombstone, you saddle up now and he heard back to the last place you seen Sam pick up his trail and follow it, but make sure you leave us a good one, so we can follow you.

Then this tall, stocky hard as nails man said something that brought everyman that works for him to his feet "I pray to god that were not too late, so from this moment on we ride for Sam Cooper, US Marshall"

The men who worked for bill Kilpatrick had never seen their boss man angry but not only could they see the anger in his face they could feel it in their souls. The men knew then that this ride would be like no other ride they had even taken. If something has happened to Sam, this would turn out to be a ride for vengeance and it would end at the end of the rope with no mercy shown,

Shorty, tombstone and Pete, had already picked out three fresh horses and were saddling them when Mr. Kilpatrick walked up to them and handed each man two boxes of ammunition and then he pointed at their Winchesters and said," make sure everything that you have is loaded all the way around and ready for use. Then he looked at his son and said," we will be no more than 30 minutes behind you, we'll do our best to catch up with you as soon as possible, but you three find Sam, now get and may God ride with you"

It took dusty and Manuel less than 30 minutes to be ready to ride, all three horses were saddled and loaded with ammunition and food along with bedrolls and each bedroll had a shotgun tied to it.

Trudeau told the two young deputies that they were going to take the train as far as they possibly could, and they headed for the railway depot to catch the next train going east. Their timing could not have been better, just as they arrived at the depot the eastbound was pulling in, Trudeau rode up to the engineer and told him what was going on, and all the engineer said was, "get your horses in the cattle car, it's empty and I'll run this thing wide open for as long as I can." It took the marshal and his two deputies less than five minutes to load their horses, the two deputies went to the dining car and Trudeau went to the engine to help the boiler stoked.

The Marshal climbed aboard the engine, grabbed a pair of gloves and a shovel and started shoveling coal, the engineer had to tell them to stop. There was no need in blowing up the boiler it had to build up a full head of a steam, and the engineer sounded the whistle and opened the throttle. The wind felt good on Trudeau's face, but he feared they were too late because moments before he had felt a cold chill on his back of his neck, in his heart and soul, Trudeau knew that the end had come just as Sam had predicted.

Klein sat and watched Sam bleed to death and laughed, then he said, "His horse looks fresh, so if one of you wants it, get it. Don't forget to get his side arm and his Winchester. Hell even get the shotgun, go through his saddlebags and get all the immunization there is , As of the night now we split up and we'll meet at the abandoned ranch, just across the border south of El Paso. There will be a posse out looking for this marshal and we best be a long way away when they find him, there is no turning back now I can guarantee you there will be no trial. Only Texas justice, and if you don't know what that is, it's a short rope in the tall tree. Now ride like your life depended on it. "Then Klein laughed. A strange eerie laugh and said, "as a matter of fact, your life does depend it." Without any discussion at all the four men mounted up and took off in four different directions leaving Sam tied to the three, the campfire still burning. And the feeling that the curse Sam had put on Klein was already working.

Mr. Kilpatrick had dispatched one of his men to go to the railhead and wait for the help that was coming from El Paso, and then lead them back to the rest of the wranglers. He figured it would take the train at least 24hours to reach the railhead, then from the railhead it would take the better part of a day to reach the red river, by then, Pete and the boys would have picked up Sam's trail and quite possibly have found Sam.

As the train sped through the dessert all Trudeau could think about was where Sam was at that very minute, he remembered Sam and his devotion to duty. His sense of humor and the fact that he wanted to live even though he believed his destiny had already been written.

The engineer told Trudeau, "Why don't you go on the back to the driving car and be with your deputies, there's nothing more you can do up here. I've got a fireman and besides, you're going to need all your strength"

Knowing that the engineer was right, Trudeau climbed up on the coal car, walked across the top of it and the top of the passenger car, then climb down a ladder to the door of the dining car and went inside. The two deputies were sitting in booth staring out the window, so intently that they didn't even noticed when Trudeau walked up, They were started back to reality when Trudeau sat down. The porter came over and asked Trudeau if he wanted anything to eat? Trudeau shook his head yes and said," whatever the special is bring all the three of us one and a large pot of coffee." Then Trudeau looked at both men and said," I know that you are feeling down and worried about Sam ,but was have to keep up your strength and keep our minds clear and focused on what has to be done. We can't look at the worst of everything we must have faith and believe that above all Sam will find some way to survive.

Trudeau knew in his mid that Sam was gone. But he had to keep up appearances for these two young deputies who had grown quite fond of Sam .he had made a great impression on these two young men and that impression would remain with them for the rest of their lives. And every time that they penned their duty badge on they would think of, Sam and remember how he worked with them, and taught them how to be a law man.

There would be no place on this earth that Alan Klein could hide that Trudeau would not find him, and he would personally see to it that this man kept his date with the hangman noose. This was a promise that Trudeau made to himself, Klein would pay for everything that he had done for every life he had taken especially, "Sam's"

The engineer had kept his word, because the train had run at full speed, only making two stops for water and one for a coal. Other than those two stops the train had not paused for anything. And as the sun came up in the East, they came up on the railhead in which the Kilpatrick rider was waiting Trudeau was out of the engine before it came to a complete stop and as the train slowed he pounded on the side of the dining car and motion for the two deputies to come out. When the train stopped the cattle car was right in front of Trudeau, so without waiting for the conductor the three men put down the ramp and led their horses off still saddled and ready to go.

The Kilpatrick rider introduced himself and said, "we've got a pretty good distance to cover, so we need to get started as soon as you gentlemen are ready"Trudeau looked at the young man said,"If you're waiting on us you're backing up"

Without anything else being said, the four men headed out Southeast, the point where they were to join up with the Kilpatrick riders was about five hours of hard riding.

Trudeau asked the rider," when was the last time that Sam was seen?" Somewhere around 3 o'clock yesterday afternoon, I think, but if you want to know exactly you'll have to talk to Pete Kilpatrick, he was riding with the marshal Cooper, when the marshal ordered him to rejoin his father and the trail drive."

After riding for about an hour, the four men get off of their horses and walked to let their horses rest for about 15 minutes, then they remounted and started off at a gallop for another hour. This continued till they cited the Kilpatrick riders, Stopping the young rider pulled his Winchester and fired three rounds into the air, the Kilpatrick riders stopped and watched as the four men headed their way at the swiftest pace the horses could muster.

Mr., Kilpatrick was the firestone to speak when the two parties met, I've got three men out trailing your Marshall when they find him one will return to us the other two was stay with Sam, and we need to keep moving, if you're no objection"

"I was about to say the same thing to you, Mr. Kilpatrick. My name is US Marshall Trudeau, these are my two deputies dusty and Manuel, now that all the niceties are over with, let's move"

For the next couple hours, all the men spread out in different direction staying within sight of each other. It was coming up on Sunset when a lone rider was seen heading in their direction, pausing till the rider got there, they waited patiently for a report that they had found Sam.

When the rider was close enough to recognize it turned out to be tombstone. When he met up with the Kilpatrick rider's tombstone looked as if he had been in the saddle for a week. Slowly and very deliberately tombstone spoke "Mr. Kilpatrick, we found Sam and it aint pretty. We found him tied to a Cottonwood, he had been beaten and then shot twice. Once in his shoulder and once through his badge into his chest. Whoever they were took his horse, his gun and left him tied. We cut him loose and wrapped him in blankets, we were unsure of whether we should go ahead and bury him or not. We're not really that far from where Pete and shortly are so let's go."

Trudeau dropped his head and took a deep breath, then looked at his two deputies, the two deputies looked back at Trudeau and dusty said." Were okay, Marshall, let's go take care of Sam"

They had ridden a little over an hour, when they saw the glow of a campfire against the night sky, tombstone said," were here Mr. Kilpatrick" and he led the way over a small ridge and to the edge of the red river where the campsite was when they arrived Trudeau, dismounted and walked over to the blanket wrapped body and uncovered Sam's face. As he looked at Sam. He swore that the monster who done this would play and he would pay with his life.

"We should take Sam back and have a nice ceremony for him. But I don't think that's possible we don't have enough salt to pack around him to keep him from deteriorating so I suggest that we bury him right here in this quiet, peaceful place. Sam would like that." Trudeau said while choking back a tear.

Two of the Kilpatrick riders had shovels with them, so without saying anything or moving very swiftly, slowly they dismounted, got their shovels and began digging a grave. one of the other riders walked over to a cotton wood reached in his saddlebags and pulled out a hatched and started making a cross to mark Sam's grave with in the meantime, Mr. Kilpatrick told one of the riders to see if he could fix a pot of coffee and he reckoned that they miss well plan on making camp here for the night.

Pete walked up to his dad and you could see the anger in his face and he asked his dad " he was my friend paw, and I want to ride with the Marshal to help bring down these monsters" Mr. Kilpatrick shook his head and pointed at Trudeau and said "ask him"

Trudeau looked at the young man stuck out his hand and said, "You were Sam's friend. As far as I'm concerned, you've earned the right to help track these bastards down and as much as I want to have a hanging party, we can't, We have to bring these men in alive, if we possibly can, you have to promise me son that you won't get gun happy and revenge Sam's death by yourself," You've got my word Marshall," Pete said, without batting an eye."

The riders took turns digging and before long, the grave was done and the men very gently without ropes picked Sam's body up and placed it in the grave very gently, one rider pulled off his jacket and placed it over Sam's face, Then they started covering Sam up each rider took his turn very gently shoveling dirt to cover Sam's body, By the time they had the grave filled the cowboy that was making a cross had finished. He then took his knife and stuck it into the campfire and burnt on the cross these words "Here lies United States Marshall

Samuel Cooper murdered by Alan Klein September 2, 1879"

Trudeau asked the young Wrangler who made the cross, if he would allow him to set the cross to Trudeau and walked with him over the grave, so he could hold the cross while Trudeau took a shovel and drove it into the ground, Trudeau had not noticed, but while this was going on the other wranglers were gathering up stones to cover Sam's grave. When they had finished as far as graves go.... It was a pretty one. Trudeau dropped to one knee and cried.

While crying, Trudeau said a prayer and thanked Sam's maker for allowing him the privilege of knowing such a fine outstanding young man.

After they had buried Sam and Mr. Kilpatrick had read from his Bible, the men all gathered around the campfire and sit quietly except for one Wrangler who got up and walked over to Trudeau reached in his pocket and said "Pete, tombstone and shortly, thought you might like to have this", pulling his hand out of his vest pocket, he handed Trudeau Sam's badge. They had not try to fix the bullet hole that was in it. The badge to them was a reminder of just how violently their friend had died and how no matter what his death had to be an example of courage, determination, honor and pride.

Trudeau took the badge, reached into his back pocket and pulled out a handkerchief and preceded to wipe the blood off of the badge, when he had finish cleaning the badge, he took the blood soaked handkerchief and stretched it out on his lap and slowly, but very precisely folded the handkerchief around the badge and placed it in his vest pocket. Then he looked up and said, "one day another man will wear this badge, and this man will avenge Sam's death. Sam himself told me that this would happen six months ago, somehow he knew how things were going to end, but he came after Klein anyway. Now it's my job to run this man down, but from what Sam said and believed will never catch this man, but someone else will, and as Sam said, this man will carry "Hell" in his right hand."

All of the men were suddenly disturbed by the sound of horses, springing to their feet, each man grabbed his Winchester drawn, and found what cover they could, Mr. Kilpatrick told his men not to fire unless fired upon. Slowly and very cautiously, the riders came into camp with their Winchesters drawn, and then a familiar sound and voice was heard. The chuck wagon and whiskers came riding into the campfire light. And as he brought his team of mules to a halt. He stood up on the chuck wagon, looked at Sam's grave and said, "What are we waiting for, let's go get these son of bitches"

Mr. Kilpatrick spoke up," not now whiskers, we can trail them in the dark, so you might as well get down and I believe that most of these wranglers could stand a good meal, if you're up to it" " in honor of Sam, I'll fix these men a supper that they'll never forget,'"" whiskers, I want you to meet a longtime friend of Sam's, this is US Marshall Trudeau, and these are their two deputies, dusty and Manuel" whiskers stuck out his hand to Trudeau and said , " any friend of Sam's is a friend of mine," He shook Trudeau's hand and then turned the two deputies and shook their hands, then he turned and walked over to Sam's grave, he stood there starring at the grave for a quite a few minutes, then he turned and with a choked voice said, " you boys did good, it's a nice grave." He then went to the back of his chuck wagon and lowered the tailgate while two of the cowboys were unlocking his mules and feeding them, he preceded to prepare supper, quietly and very determined, whiskers set about preparing the best meal that he would ever fix. Whiskers stepped back from the wagon turned and motioned for Mr. Kilpatrick to come over there, when Kilpatrick got there whiskers whispered something to him. Mr. Kilpatrick put his hand on whiskers shoulder and said, "I don't see anything wrong with that, go ahead."

Whiskers reached into a bag of meal and pulled out a bottle of whiskey and said," Sam gave me this bottle for medicinal purposes, so I figure it's only right that we toast him and his life, so get your cups, gentlemen and form a line." Whiskers, then reached and got a cup poured a shot in it and walked over to Sam's grave and set the cup down next to the cross and said, "You drink first Sam" Then he reached and got the cup and turned it upside down on Sam's grave, took his hand and scooped out a hole, the buried the cup in the grave.

The old man was hurting, you could see it in his face and in the way he moved, but more than hurt he was angry, the kind of anger that has got many a man Lynched, Trudeau was glad that the old man was not going with him, simply because in his frame of mind, he could and he would persuade a bunch of riders to string somebody up, and that would dishonor Sam, and that was one thing that would never happen.

Dusty and Manuel asked whiskers if he could use some help, he smiled, shook his head yes, he then told the two deputies what he needed done in the meantime, Mr. Kilpatrick had sent men out to gather wood to keep the fire going and build up a bed of coals so whiskers could cook.

Mr. Kilpatrick looked over at Trudeau and ask, "Can you recognize Sam's horse?" "Yes sir, I sure can, I helped him pick it out." Then Pete said, "If we can find the man riding that horse we can force him to tell us where Klein is, can't we?"

Trudeau looked at the young man, and with a very Stem face and voice, he said, "Not only can we, I can guarantee that whoever rides that horse, will talk sooner or later he will talk."

The wranglers had already started unsaddling their horses, and picketing them in a manner that they could graze and get to the bank of the red river to drank. They had spread out their bedrolls and were leaning back, relaxing, but very few were talking, mostly they just stared at Sam's grave. Trudeau noticed that a few of the wranglers were setting with their backs to the campfire and reading the bible.

All of a sudden one of the late arriving wranglers jumped up and said, "Holy smoke had done forgot to give you this boss." The wrangler then handed Mr. Kilpatrick a piece of paper and an envelope. "That's all right, I had completely forgotten about it myself, that just goes to show you that friendship means a whole lot more than money could ever mean" without opening the envelope. He just folded it, and placed it in the inside pocket of his vest. Then he preceded to read the piece of paper that the wrangler had handed him, and with a smile and a chuckle he folded it also and placed it with the envelope.

It seemed that the tension of finding Sam and the events leading up to it were starting to subside, as the men were starting to talk and even a few would laugh every so often. A lot of the men were cleaning there weapons and after cleaning them, they we're reloaded. One of the men asked Mr. Kilpatrick if they were all going after the men who killed Sam, Mr. Kilpatrick was quick to say "no" "why not, the wrangler ask?"

because if we got after them men in the frame of mind that we are in it would not be posse but a Lynch mob, and as Marshall Trudeau said that would be a disgrace and something that Sam would not want, so were going to let the Marshall do his job, and we'll do ours."

After they had finished their supper, Trudeau told dusty and Manuel that they had better get some sleep, because they were going to be travelling early in the morning, just as soon as it was light enough to see, Mr. Kilpatrick spoke up and said , "That's why I'm letting my son go with you. He is a very accomplished tracker. One of them at my ranch, that takes care of my horses is a full-blooded Comanche, and he has taught Pete ever since he was big enough to walk how to track and read sign" Trudeau looked over at the young man and said ," when daylight breaks I want to ride"

Whiskers spoke up and said, "I'll have breakfast ready for you in enough time so you can eat and still be in the saddle at sun up" By the way whiskers that was one mighty fine supper, the kind of supper that Sam would really have enjoyed." Trudeau said, "I also understand that Sam really liked your fried dried apples pies." I'd give anything Marshall if I could fixing one more for him."

The old man turned and walk away, the next thing that Trudeau knew was whiskers had poured him a cup of coffee and had walked over to Sam's grave and sit down in solitary and it seemed as if whiskers, was talking to Sam -----"maybe he was."

Most all of the wranglers had turned in for the night and it was extremely quiet in the camp, the kind of quiet that would allow a man to think. As Trudeau stretched out in his bedroll, He thought back to the day he first met Sam. He was a Texas Ranger, and mighty proud of it. He was the type of a man who didn't believe in putting off the inevitable, but believed in facing everything head on, Reaching into the inside pocket of his vest Trudeau pulled out Sam's badge and as he lay staring at the badge in his mind, he heard these words " don't worry, I'll always have your back," it was as if Sam had been sitting beside him and made that statement, it shocked Trudeau, so much that he sat up straight and looked around, there was a cold chill that hit his back and his neck and he knew then that Sam would ride with him from now on.

It took a few minutes for Trudeau to get his composure back in the meantime, he continued to clean Sam's badge. He figured as soon as he got to a blacksmith's shop, he would have the blacksmith's smooth out the bullet hole, but not take it away, not repair it, just straightened out the ragged edges around the hole ,Studying the badge for a few minutes Trudeau wrapped it back up in his bloody handkerchief and replaced it in his vest.

He happened to glance over at dusty and Manuel and they were already asleep, Sam would have said they were sleeping the sleep of the innocent and he would have been right.

Mr. Kilpatrick did not think they would venture back to the campsite, but just to be on the safe side. He set up nighthawks into hour shifts, that way everybody could get a good night sleep. He had already made up his mind that tomorrow morning he would take the rest of the wranglers and head back to his ranch, with the understanding, that if Trudeau run into trouble ,his son would hightail it to the ranch for help, he could also tell that from the way dusty and Manuel wore their weapons that they had been taught how to use them very efficiently, and then there was Trudeau, a seasoned hard –nosed United States Marshall that had in his time been a hard man to handle and without a doubt had put a slug in quite a few men and before this was over would probably put a few slugs and quite a few more men.

Trudeau and Kilpatrick finally realized that they were the only two still awake .So they too decided to call it a night, with a simple, "See you in the morning," Both men turned in.

Trudeau had not been asleep long when he began to dream, it was as if him and Sam were having a cup of coffee and talking the way they used to, he dreamed of the times when Sam would laugh and pull a prank on somebody all in fun. He dreamed of the night. That he and Consuela shared with Lolita and Sam, drinking and dancing and laughing and how full of life, everyone seemed to be at that moment.

He also in his dreams seen just how fast with a 45 that Sam was, very few men could match his speed but what made him extremely good was how accurate he could be. The dreams that Trudeau was having become so real that he could have sworn it Sam that woke him up. But it wasn't, it was whiskers and breakfast was ready. He had already woke up Dusty and Manuel, Pete was already sitting at the campfire with a plate and a cup of coffee Trudeau was not as young as he once was so if took him a few minutes to get the kinks out of his body from sleeping on the ground, but he still enjoyed the outdoors and the rugged life.

Glancing over at the horses, Trudeau noted that all four horses were saddled and ready to go. They had been fed and evidently had been taken down to the water 'sedge to get a good drank because all four horses' front legs we're wet.

Walking over to the campfire Trudeau sat down beside Pete and ask, "How long have you been up Pete?" without looking up, Pete answered." I took the last nighthawk shift, so I've been up about two hours, I hope you don't mind, but I took the privileged of saddling everyone's horse after I fed them and watered them, I just wanted to be ready Marshall," Well, all I can say is thanks, and as soon as the sky starts to gray up, we'll be riding, I take it you're going to ride point?" Yes sir, it will be a whole lot easier for me to track with you and your men behind me, than in front of me"

There was not much more business to talk about, So Trudeau started asking questions about where the Kilpatrick's came from originally. And how long they had been in central Texas? It seemed that the more Trudeau learned about the Kilpatrick clan, The more he wanted to know about this family, There was some stories told by Mr., Kilpatrick about how much trouble his sons used to get into trying to do things they didn't know how to do, Like the first time that Pete decided he was going to ride a six month old steer, well, after the steer had thrown him four or five times. He decided that being a rodeo cowboy was not in his future, he left that steer alone, after that.

The sky had started to turn gray and there was the beginning of orange showing over the Ridge to the East, So, Trudeau stood up, put down his coffee cup and stuck out his hand once more to Mr. Kilpatrick and said, "If there is any way possible. I will bring these men in or see that they are bought in, and I'll keep your son as safe as I possibly can, and out of the line of fire in case it comes down to that "you take care my friend and I promise you, from time to time somebody from my ranch will visit Sam and tend to his grave."

With the sun slowly peeking over the ridge to the east, and three anxious young men already mounted on their horses, Trudeau took one last look at grave of his friend and made this promise, "They will be brought to justice Sam, if it's the last thing I do, they will pay the ultimate price. "Walking over to his horse and slowly mounting the two young deputies could see a trickle of a tear running down Trudeau's cheek, and it was then that dusty and Manuel understood just how deep the friendship of these two men had been,

Trudeau looked over at Pete, nodded his head, and with the look of determination, and pain said, "Okay, Mr. Tracker start tracking."

As the sun rise higher in the morning sky. It warmed Trudeau's back and it reminded him of his dream and what Sam had told him. The words kept echoing in Trudeau's mind "Don't worry, I've got your back." He felt a smile because of Sam the future was looking better already.

Pete was tracking at a pretty good pace and whoever this rider was he was not varying from the direction that he started out taking he was making a beeline for the Mexican border, They had tracked for the better part of the morning when Pete pulled up and dismounted, picking up a shotgun . He turned and walked back to Trudeau and handed the gun to him. Trudeau smiled and told Pete "This shotgun came from my office, Sam was carrying the shotgun, now we know for sure that the man we're trailing is riding Sam's horse. "Then he looked very defiantly at Pete, "Don't lose him son."

Don't worry Marshall, there ain't no way in hell he's going to get away." With new energy and determination. Pete swung back up into the saddle, and like a bloodhound he was on the trail and moving quickly.

For the rest of the day and rite up till dark they kept up the pace and just as darkness was about to fall they seems the lights of a small prairie town in the distance, it was then that Pete turned to Trudeau, pointed at the town . I'll bet everything I own that he's in that town."

The closer they got to the town. They heard the rollicking music of a honky-tonk piano playing and the loudness of people talking coming from a small saloon, as the four men pulled up in front of the saloon, Trudeau was very quickly down off of his horse. There were three horses led to the hitching post, and one of the horses was Sam's.

Trudeau patted the horse on his neck and the horse seem to recognize Trudeau as he said, "Whiskey, I'll be taking you home soon."

Manuel walked up to a window and looked in, then turned around and motioned for dusty and he looked through the window, also turning to Trudeau Manuel said, "The man wearing the flat brimmed hat and the blue denim shirt is one of the two men that we arrested in Abilene. They were in the jail, along with Lane when Ranger Thompson was killed.

Trudeau walked up and locked through the window, his eyes narrowed and he gritted his teeth as he said, "That son of a bitch is wearing Sam's gun. He turned to dusty and Manuel once again, telling them that he was going alone.

Dusty and Manuel both shook their heads," no" He was our friend too." Trudeau told Pete to stay out with the horses, and stay out of the line of fire, then he turned and followed by dusty and Manuel walked through the open.

Door of the saloon. The man that was wearing Sam's gun never turned around and never looked up as Trudeau stopped at the bar on one side of him and dusty stopped on the other side, while Manuel stood directly behind him.

Trudeau ordered a shot of whiskey, downed it. Then turned to the man and very quietly reached in his pocket and pulled out Sam's badge unfolding the handkerchief he laid it on the bar in front of the man, as the outlaw stared at the badge he said, "I didn't kill him, Klein did," " Makers no difference Trudeau said, you were there and you didn't stop it. And for that I will see you hang. You don't murder a United States Marshall, and walk away. Now, where is Klein headed? And where are you supposed to meet up with him??"

"Klein is headed for the ranch that he was raised on, it's been abandoned since his parents died, but he still owns it. He says it's more of a ghost town now than a ranch, but he uses it from time to time to hold up anyway were supposed to meet as fast as we can because Klein wants to score one more bank and then head into the New Mexico territory, From there, he says we can split up and go to Colorado, California, but if we want to live we need to stay out of the dessert, I think Klein is planning on Colorado."

"Where were you planning on going?" Trudeau asked, "I was thinking about getting as deep into Mexico as I possibly could, maybe even South America believe it or not. I'm afraid of Klein," he's crazy,"

Trudeau said, "I should hang you right now, but I'm not going to but if you're planning to go to Mexico you're going to have to walk because I'll be talking Sam's horse, I hope you can find another then Trudeau squared around and looked into the man's eyes, then told him to unbuckle his gun belt.

For some reason or another, the man thought that he could fight his way out, so as unbuckled the gun belt with his left hand, his right hand slapped the butt of Sam's 45 and in a flash. There was the roar as Trudeau's 45, backwards, never knowing when he hit the floor, Trudeau pitched a $20 gold piece on the bar and told the bartender it was to pay someone to put this man in the ground.

Picking up Sam's gun belt and removing Sam's 45 from the man's hand, Trudeau turned and walked back out the door, He turned to Pete and said, "Son, there's no need of you going any further, I want you to go back and felt your dad that we got one of the men who killed Sam and we know who actually pulled the trigger, dusty, Manuel and I are going to back to El Paso, and when I get there I will notify every law enforcement agency from El Paso West that Alan Klein is wanted for the murder of a United States Marshall."

Trudeau, shook the young man's hand and told him if he or his family ever needed the law just let him know and he would be there.

Before Pete turned his horses, He looked at Trudeau and promise him "I will see to it sir, That Marshall Cooper's grave is well tended. I think my mama and my sister's would enjoy planting some flowers and maybe sewing some grass seed. I'll make sure that Sam is not forgot.

Trudeau walked over and untied whiskey from the hitching rail. Handed the reins to Manuel and as he stepped up into the saddle. He said "Let's get out of this town, we can still ride for a couple of hours before we make camp...

Manuel took and tied the reins together and hung them over the saddle horn, and attached a lead rope, to whiskey's bridal, He wanted whiskey to feel like Sam was still in the saddle and he would make him easier to lead, Whiskey seem to know what was going on, ,his ear were all perked up in his eyes were bright and full of life and as they left town whiskey was not trailing them he was right beside Manuel and Trudeau felt as if Sam was on that horse foolish I guess, but that was the way, Trudeau felt and it made Trudeau feel safer. Even Manuel and dusty seemed more at ease. Maybe Sam had spoken to them too. It would be a blessing if he did. The three law men had ridden. I guess 10 miles when they came up on the stand of cottonwoods that had a spring Trudeau said, "This looks like a good place, let's call it a quits for today. Dusty you and Manuel take care of the horses, and I'll get some coffee and a fire going. I think there's some bacon and some beans in Sam's saddlebags. As soon as you get the horses took care of if you don't mind bring the saddle bags to me."

Manuel and dusty unsaddled the horses and put their saddlers around where Trudeau was starting a fire. They had hobbled the horses, so they could graze and drank, but not run… rolling out their bedrolls, dusty rolled out Trudeau's and his. Manuel rolled out his bedroll, then looked at Sam's saddle and for the first time Trudeau saw emotion in the young men's face, the longer he stood and looked at the saddle, the sadder his eye's got, and finally, the evidence of a fear.

Trudeau broke the silence by saying," don't worry about that bedroll, Sam's sleeping on a big while fluffy cloud tonight, no more hard ground for critters crawling under the blanket with you, and no more rocks under your blanket, Sam is in good hands."

This didn't seem to soothe Manuel too much because he turned and said to Trudeau," how am I going to explain this to my mother, and Lolita? How do I tell them that the man they both cared about, in different ways, is not coming back?! You tell me that Marshall explain it to me "

"You leave that part to me son, that's the cross I have to bear not you I should have not let Sam go by himself. I should have went with, and by rights that should be me in that grave. You get right down to it. I believe it's my fault Sam's gone, and I alone will have to answer to the people of El Paso."

The campsite was quiet in a while, or hear the rattling of a tin skillet you would have never known that anyone was in this campsite.

Dusty was the first one to break the silence, When right out of the blue he asked," I wonder what judged walker is going to have to say about all this? Him and Sam had gotten to be real good friends. Did you know that those two played checkers together? And I know for a fact that Sam used to beat his pants off. The judged used to swear and tell Sam that if he didn't lose once in a while he was going to put him in a jail for disturbing the peace, and then they both would laugh and the judge would offer Sam a drank out of that shiny flask that he always carried in his coat .I used to enjoy just settles watching them, they were like a couple of old school buddies that never grew up "If you don't mind Marshall, that's the way I want to remember Sam"

"There are things about Sam that I want to remember to, such as the way he really enjoyed a real cold beer, or talking about his parents. His brothers and how he hadn't seen his sister since his parents died. He loved to talk about Ben Johnson and how the man had been both a big brother and a father to him, how he had taught him, how to become a ranger, how he went about installing into Sam, the devotion to knowing the difference between right and wrong, yeah... I'll have my own way of remembering of Sam, just like Manuel will have his own way , but there's one thing for sure, all three of us now has a duty and I count it a privilege to make sure that whiskey is well taken care of. We must take him out for a ride any chance we get, that horse loved Sam and I'm quite sure that he will miss his gentle hand."

" Dusty spoke up and said ,I sure am going to be glad to get back home, to tell you the truth I miss judged walker and his cantankerous attitude toward just about everything, I firmly believe that man lives just to agitate somebody."

Trudeau, shook his finger at dusty and said, "you know, I'm inclined to agree with you, the old judged could piss off a preacher, and he would if he got half a chance and you can believe that."

"I wonder if the new Ranger will want to keep me on, Manuel ask."

"Don't worry about anything like that Manuel I will personally asked the next ranger to allow you to stay, I'm pretty sure that the next Ranger will want you to stay, but just in case, they don't keep the ranger posted open there in El Paso, I've got the feeling that I'm going to need another deputy, I really think I should have two deputies anyway, don't you?

Deep in his heart, Trudeau knew that it was going to take a long time to get used to Sam not being there, the one bright spot that Trudeau felt he had to look forward to Sam's prediction that another would take his place and that he would finish the job that Sam had started. Trudeau was looking forward to meeting this man, and comparing him to Sam.

The three men had their supper, and had finished off a complete pot of coffee and the weariness of the day was starting to take effect .Dusty had leaned back against his saddle and had fallen asleep.

Manuel was not sleeping with his saddle, but he had spread out his bedroll and had his head resting on Sam's saddle, He also had fallen asleep.

Trudeau looked up at the stars and said "You made a hell of an impression on those two young men Sam, and I don't think they'll forgetting you ever, I hope that you will watch over them, and protect them, they deserve it."

Trudeau stocked up the fire, so that there would still be some live coals in the morning, at least enough to allow to start another fire and make coffee, Leaning back again his saddle Trudeau wondered if Sam would come to him again in his dreams......he hope he would.

CHAPTER 7

The three men were awakened very gently the next morning by the warmth of the sun shining on their faces. They had slept without moving all night and past dawn, it was the first time that Trudeau had ever done that he felt much energized and much rested, could it be that Sam had stoodguard all night. The horses were extremely gentle and moving very slowly. They seem to be enjoying themselves, just grazing and getting a drink of water occasionally.

There were still coals in the fire pit, so all Trudeau had to do was throw some wood in it and wait for it to catch, in the meantime, with the water already in the coffee pot, all he had to do was put the coffee in, with the touch of salt and set it on a stone close to the fire and let it boil. While Trudeau was getting the fire started, dusty and Manuel were saddling the horses, and rolling up the bedrolls and securing them.

The two young deputies seemed extremely spry as they were laughing and joking about what they were going to do when they got back to El Paso and as they called civilization. Thinking back to a time in his younger years when he reacted the same way. Trudeau thought of the first time that he met Sam, and they went and had a beer together and talked as if they were both going to live forever as far as Trudeau was concerned Sam now would live forever in his thoughts and in his prayers and occasionally in his dreams.

Sam had been 36 when he was killed, Trudeau was already 51 and soon it would be time for him to retire. It was going to be quite difficult to walk away from the law and his badge, especially because he had no one to share his golden years with, Trudeau had been married when he was young, but she could accept being the wife of someone who got shot at almost everyday and when his daughter came along. His wife decided that she could go back to Virginia where her family is for safety. But instead she walk right into the middle of the war between the states. And most of her family were killed. He had received word that his wife passed away, some six years ago and there was no trace about his daughter. He could only hope that she had gotten married and that was the only reason why he couldn't trace her name. Maybe someday she would get curious enough to trace his down, if only to ask him why her parents separated.

The coffee was ready and the three men enjoyed a couple of cups apiece, then look the remainder of the coffee and put out the campfire.

Dusty and Manuel were smiling and joking and Trudeau asked them, "Why? Dusty answered, "the way, I've got it figured Marshall is that by dark tonight, we should be back in El Paso and I don't know about you, but as far as I'm concerned this has been a nightmare and I want it to end. So when we get back don't look for me for a couple of days because I fully intend to get dog down, loop legend drunk," Manuel spoke up and said ,"what do you mean you? Don't you mean we are going to get drunk?"

Trudeau studied a minute, nodded his head, "Sounds like the right thing to do, I wonder if the judge would like to join us? Maybe Consuela and Lolita would like to join us too" Maybe they could all have a drink for Sam and celebrate his life. And at the same time believing in Sam and believing that he is not dead, just on a higher plan,

With no further discussion the three men saddled up and with Sam's horse in tow, they started out with the sun to their back and fully intended to ride until the sun was hiding its face behind the rolling hills that bordered the Rio Grande. The longer they rode the more anxious all three men seem to get. Everytime they would come to a ranch or a small settlement they would stop and water their horses, allowing them to rest, while the horses were resting all three men would ask questions, trying to find out if there had been any strangers riding by in a hurry toward El Paso. Everytime dusty would end his conversation with someone by asking just how far it was to El Paso. The last place they stopped told dusty that it was a little over 20 miles to El Paso.

The last place the last place they stopped was a rather large ranch owned by the Arnett family. Trudeau had heard about this family, but he had never met anyone of them so they spent a little extra time passing the time of day and allowing the horses to rest completely.

Mr. Arnett noticed that whiskey didn't have a rider and he asked why, Manuel then told Mr. Arnett the story of Sam Cooper, almost breaking down in tears once or twice Manuel finally finished by saying, "Sam Cooper will be a legend as long as I live. He was a brave man, and honest man, and he believed in second chances. Two of those second chances played a part in Sam's murder, and those two men are now in hell"

Mrs. Arnett told Manuel that he should take a lesson from this Sam Cooper, She told him that you could not live your life second guessing everything that happened sometimes you just have to have faith in your fellow man, she also told Manuel that if he really wanted to keep Sam alive, then live his life doing things that he felt Sam would approve of, and be proud.

Trudeau told Mr. Arnett that he had really enjoyed the visit, but that they really needed to be on their way, they wanted to be in El Paso by nightfall, and they were going to have to push it in order to do that, Mr. Arnett, shook hands with all three men. Mrs. Arnett gave all three men a hug and said, "May the good Lord ride with you and keep you safe until we meet again."

Riding away from the Arnett ranch, Dusty told Trudeau, "I like those people, they seem like a God-fearing family.

There couldn't have been any more than a couple of dozen words said after that, each man kept scanning the horizon for any sign of home, or for signs of any riders that seem to be in a hurry. Everything was going fine until Manuel noticed that whiskey's ears were perked up and he was lagging behind. Manuel brought his horse to a halt and just sat and watched whiskey and looked in the direction that the horse was looking. The horse had sensed something, so Manuel decided to check it out. Trudeau and dusty seen Manuel and whiskey make a turn to the south, so being curious they followed. They hadn't gone very far till they seem a horse that had evidently gone lame. Manuel rode up to the horse and dismounted walked up to the horse and raised its left front foot. It seemed that the horse had stepped on a small cactus and had embedded a few needles in the soft part of his hoof. Taking a pair of pliers out of his saddlebags. Manuel preceded to pull out the needles and after that the horse seem to be okay. Not wanting to leave the horse behind, he didn't!!

Handing the reins of the second horse to dusty, marshal continued leading whiskey and the three men continued on their way to El Paso .It was going to be dark or a little after sunset when they arrived, but it didn't matter. The next time they got out of the saddle. They would be home.

Manuel got up beside Trudeau and said, "Marshal, this has been one hard trip, and it's not something I wish to do over again, so I have spent a lot of time thinking about something I haven't quite made up my mind yet, but I will soon."

I know Manuel that you are thinking about turning in your badge, and I don't blame outdoes Dusty feel the same way that you do?"

"Yes sir, he and I have discussed it a lot and I think he was pretty much made up his mind, but I think that he is afraid he will be letting you down and leaving you with no protection or anyone to watch your badge."

"Is that the way you feel too?"

"I guess in a way, yes. Keep thinking about Sam, and what would he do? What would his solution to this problem be? And what do the two of us need to take into consideration before we make a decision? I really don't know which way to turn Marshall"

Trudeau was silent, for just a moment and then he answered, "Sam would tell you that if your heart is not in it, then don't do it. If your heart's not in it. You can't do your best, if you and Dusty want to turn in your badges when we reach town, then I have no problem with accepting them, but make sure that it's you that wants to turn your badge in, and not your memory of Sam, and What he went through before you died."

With that Trudeau urged his horse on, and for the next couple of hours, He stayed in front of the two deputies, just to give them a chance to talk things over and decide exactly what they wanted to do.

The sun had gone down and the darkness was starting to fall when they topped a small rise and seen the lights of El Paso .Just for a moment the three men paused and the reality that this may be the last time these three men would ride together and set in.

Dusty had been engaged for over a year and after what happened to Sam. Dusty decided if he was going to die there was going to be someone there to hold his hand and say I love you. So, reaching up, he took the badged off and handed it to Trudeau and said, "my last act as a deputy will be to take whiskey and this other horse to the livery stable and make sure that whiskey gets the best care and attention that can be generated. I'm sorry Marshall, but I don't want to die before I've ever had a chance to live want kids, I want a wife and I want my own little piece of ground."

Manuel rode up to the other side of Trudeau and handed him his badge saying, "This is no reflection on you Marshall, but this job was fun till we seen the gruesome part of his job, and felt the sadness of losing a friend can't stop thinking of Sam out there in his grave in the middle of nowhere all alone, and that is not the way that I want to end up do not know how my mother is going to take my quitting as deputy, or how Lolita will react when she finds out that Sam is gone. I appreciate you offering to tell my mom and my sister about Sam, but I believe that is my piece. I was his deputy, and I really don't think that I could be anyone else's.

Finishing what he had to say Manuel started toward the lights of El Paso. Without looking back at Trudeau or dusty. But focusing on what lay in the future for him and his family, and wondering how long it would be before he could see a grave and not think of Sam.

As they rode into town there seem to be a lot of excitement there were all kinds of people in the street surrounding the bank. Everyone seemed excited to see Trudeau and the deputies, but everyone started at the two empty saddles finally, the judge showed up and the first thing he said was, "Where's Sam?" without hesitating, Trudeau said, "Sam's dead murdered by Alan Klein"

"That man has been busy, him and some of his boys just robbed the bank and killed five people, two men and a child. They were all shot point –blank for no reason just killed in cold blood."

"Just as soon as I can get to the telegraph office badge. I will send out a message to every law enforcement in New Mexico territory, Arizona territory and Colorado territory, do you think I should make it wanted dead or alive?"

The judged answered, "No sir, I want this son of a bitch in my courtroom. For the two men and two women, I would probably sentence him to life without parole. But for the child, I will hang him and enjoy every minute of it, do you know the Arnett's?"

Yes Sir, I just met then in person not long ago Judge Trudeau answered."

"Well, one of the women was the Arnett's daughter, but what really makes it bad is the little girl was the Arnett's granddaughter don't think they have been notified yet, but some of their hands are in town. And I imagine it won't be long until they know, Go do your job Marshal, let's catch this son of a bitch."

"I guess you two were right. Trudeau said. "I reckon it is time to quit but not until this man answers for everything he's done in the past 30 days. So if you two want to quit, that's okay with me. But I can't, this is one thing I have to finish"

Dusty spoke up and said, "My fiancée had waited for over a year, I don't think a couple weeks more will hurt, give me back my badge."

Without any hesitation Manuel stuck out his hand and Trudeau gladly handed both of these men their badges back then he said, "Now, gentlemen. You have you just made Sam Cooper very proud and me too. We've got a job to do. It may take a little while, but it will come to an end. You two go ahead and take care of the horses, while I go to the telegraph office and I'll meet you back at my office.

The two young men took the Marshal's horse, the stray horse, and whiskey, There was no smile on their faces as they slowly rode up the street to the livery.

When Trudeau got to the telegraph office... the telegram he sent was short and sweet, "Wanted, alive for six counts of murder and bank robbery Alan Klein, reward $10,000. He then instructed the telegraph operator to send it to every law enforcement agency within 1000 miles in any direction, including Mexico. On his way back to his office he stopped by the newspaper office and instructed the editor to make up a wanted poster stating the same as the telegram did, and he wanted 100 copies put on every stage leaving El Paso in any direction and specifically Arizona, New Mexico, Colorado, Oklahoma and Kansas.

There was nothing that could be done now, but mourn the dead and wait for the living to find Alan Klein.

For the next three weeks things were quite peaceful in El Paso, except for the fact of having to attend five funerals and one memorial service. Ben Johnson had been ordered, by the main office of the Texas Rangers to close the Ranger Station in El Paso and move that post to Abilene, Texas to cover the loss of ranger Thompson. This left only Trudeau. Dusty and Manuel. So the town council voted to elect a sheriff and hire four deputies if and when they had to leave town to pursue outlaws. Doing this insured that there would be law enforcement no matter what in the town of El Paso. This was one move by the town Council that Trudeau agreed with, and so did dusty and Manuel.

Then one day, as Trudeau sat in his office going through wanted poster. The young man that worked as a runner for the telegraph office came busting in on Trudeau and handed him an envelope. It was from the country Sheriff in Denver, Colorado and it simply stated, "Klein in custody, please send someone to transport back to El Paso, without a minute hesitation, Trudeau was up and headed for the judges office and handed him the envelope .The judged open the envelope and his face went pale with anger and he said. "I don't give a strikers dam how you get it done, but get that murdering son of a bitch back here."

"The only way I know to do this is, do it myself, and the fastest way to do it will be for me to ride my horse. The stage will take too long, and by riding I can shave at least a week off of the time it will take to get there .So if you will judged need you to send a reply to this telegram and notify them that I am on my way. Dusty and Manuel can watch my office until the Sheriff is elected and deputies are hired. Then if they still want to turn in their badges tell them it's okay, will you do that for me judge?" Yes sir, I most certainly will."

When Trudeau got back to his office, Dusty and Manuel were there, but they were not the rollicking joyful young men that they used to be ,Their faces were drawn, and they looked even older than their true age, so Trudeau sat down and explain to them what was going on, and then he asked, "If you two gentlemen will keep this office open while I'm gone, it will greatly appreciated, and upon my return If you still want to turn your badges, I won't have any objection and if they get the sheriff elected and his deputies hired before I return, and you don't want to wait as long as there is law enforcement in El Paso, then you're free to go. No matter what you choose to do, I want you to know that you are to find deputies, and I'm proud that you have chosen to work with me.

I will be leaving first thing in the morning on my way to Denver to pick up Allen Klein and transport him back here to stand trial. Your job will be an easy one. Just keep the doors open and take any messages that comes from a or ask the judge if he will move his office here if he will then you will be free to go on with your lives, with my thanks." Trudeau knew that by Sunday these two young spirited men would embark on the journey to start a new future and life.

Back in Abilene town Ben Johnson was opening the new Rangers station and was being greeted with enthusiasm by the people in the community. As all of the congratulations was going on. There was a young man just coming out of the telegraph office and he wondered what all the commotion was about. Without really knowing why he walked up to Ben Johnson and asked what was going on, Ben answered him by saying, "I guess you heard about the ranger been murdered sometime back? Well we're opening the rangers post in Abilene."

"That's sounds like a good thing, I hope everything goes good for whoever takes the post over, but as for me, I won't be here to see it. I've just been offered a job at the Michigan River Ranch in Colorado to break horses for the summer. I've always wanted my own little spread and this will enable me to make the money to pay for 200 acres of my own. So, I'll be leaving in the morning, I'm really sorry ranger to miss all the festivities, but this is a chance of a lifetime and I can't pass it up."

"I don't blame you son, your young and healthy and from the looks of you, strong as an ox, so take my advice and pursue your dreams because you never know just when life will end. I had a good friend who put the law above everything else, and he died at a young age......alone"

"I don't intend to let that happen to me ranger, I'm going to break these horses, then I'm going to buy me a piece of land back close to here and these I am going to find ,e a woman that's want a whole bunch of kids. And I'm going to leave my mark on this land."

The Ranger found this young man very interesting, so they stood and talked for quite a while and the more the ranger talk to this stranger, the more he liked him, He had an Outlook on life that you don't find very often, especially in young people, he seemed to have an understanding of the problems that can pop up all of a sudden as you go through life. This young man had plans and dreams that he was determined to fulfill. There was another young man that looked at life the same way, but he failed to act on it, and it turned out that he waited too long to pursue his dreams, although he did leave one hell of a legacy and a reputation that any man who wears the badge will recognize and envy for as long as law enforcement exist "Samuel James Cooper" A legend!!

Finally this young man told Johnson that he needed to get back to the ranch where he had been working and get ready to start travelling toward Colorado in the morning, So he and Johnson, shook hand and he started off down the street when Johnson hollered at him and ask, "By the way son, if and when you do come back and buy that land and find that woman. It's going to be hard for me to know, unless you tell me your name, "The young man turned back to face the Ranger and with a great big smile and the look of a man who knew what he wanted and was willing to go get it. He said, "My name is Matthew Rivers and I'll make sure to look you up Ranger, when I get back!!

The Ranger felt an unusual breeze blow over the back of his neck, unusual because of the coolness he felt, it was almost as if someone had placed a wet towel on the back of his neck. Needless to say this cause some cold chills on his back, Needless to say he didn't dwell on it very long because he himself had to get ready trip to Denver, and the first meeting with the man who murdered Sam Cooper.

Ben Johnson had been a Ranger for a quite few years, he had captured quite few dangers men, He had transported from one point to another many a hard-core outlaw but, this would be the only one that he was really going to enjoy bringing back to El Paso to be tried and quite possibly hung, The one thing that Ben was going to make sure of is that Alan Choctaw Klein was hung with a brand new rope.

Suddenly been gad the urge for a good hot cup of coffee and a friendly conversation with Mrs. Consuela. She was (Ben Guessed) in her late 40's or very early 50's, but no matter she still had the figure of a young woman and a lot of beauty in her face, she was the one person in this town that Ben could talk to and be completely honest with Consuela had proven many times to re-rent that room, but she had said that she was not ready to open that room up again. Sam and Consuela had developed a very strong friendship just in a short time that Sam had been in El Paso. She like a man who believed in saying what he meant, and with Sam he always meant what he said. It was plain to see that she missed her friend.

Ben walked into the restaurant, sat down at a table in the corner and it was as if Consuela had read his mind, because she immediately picked up a pot of coffee and 2 cups, when she reached the table she said to Ben, "Do you mind if I join you?" I have been on my feet since about 4:30 this morning and my feet are killing me."

Proud to have the company, Ben said."

The first thing out of Consuela's mouth was a question about whether he was going to go along with Sam being buried on the banks of the Red river, or if he was going to try to bring Sam's body back to El Paso.

It was not a subject that Ben Johnson was at ease discussing but out of respect for Consuela he said. "I have already asked the judge for a signed order to do just that, it's my understanding that Marshall Trudeau is the one that has to ask for it simply because Sam was no longer a Ranger, but a US Marshall, anyway the judged said he would take care of getting a written Trudeau is ask for that request, he will probably write it out immediately it's my understanding that Sam and Trudeau had become very good friends.

"When are you leaving for dinner? Consuela ask"

"I kind of figured I would get an early start in the morning, but just in case someone is listening that shouldn't be. I have kept it mainly to myself I'm not going to take the train, or a stagecoach fully intend to ride my horse every step of the way. I haven't made any plans about how I'm going to bring Klein back I guess I'll just play it by ear."

"Well Ben, I want you to promise me that you're going to be extremely careful. It's my understanding that Klein was the only one out of his gang that was captured. That means that all the rest of them are still out there. And you know they're going to try to break their boss out, either that or they'll be waiting somewhere along the trail for you. And it's my understanding that they don't have any qualms about shooting someone in the back. "While Consuela was saying that she reached over and touched Ben's arm, then she continued by saying, "I don't believe in my heart could stand losing another close friend. So damn, you promise me that you'll be careful!

Ben smiled a very warm smile and said. "Don't you worry about me, I'm just too damn set in my ways for anyone to sneak up on me. After all I have been at this job for a long time, maybe it's time for me to retire, I'll have to think about that."

Then puzzled lock came over his face and said, "I just met a young man who is going to Denver to break horses. He plans to make enough money to buy him about 200 acres to farm, and his plans includes finding him alive that once a house full of children. The more I think about it. Sounds like a pretty good life." Then he looked at Consuela and said "you wouldn't be interested in a deal like that, would you?

Hahaha, "I am too old to even think about something like that, and Ben Johnson, so are you" Consuela said.

Still I wish that young fellow all the luck in the world. He seems to have an awful bright outlook on life."

Consuela got up from the table, smiled at Ben and said "my feet feel a whole lot better I guess I had best get back to work, you take care of yourself Ben Johnson!!!

Ben finished his cup of coffee and started to get up from the table and just about that time that young stranger walk through the door that he had met outside. So, Ben motioned for him ,so he was kind of wanting to have a little conversation to go along with his supper, So Matthew thought to himself ,"It can't hurt to be seen at a table with a Texas Ranger."

Ben looked up at the young man and said, I'm sorry son, I guess I must be getting feebleminded, but I can't remember what you told me your name was."

"Matthew Rivers, but most everybody just calls me Matt"

Immediately Ben motioned for Consuela to bring a fresh pot of coffee and another cup to the table, when she arrived Matt looked up at her and ask."What's the special for tonight Mrs. Salazar?"

"Please call me Consuela, Mrs. Salazar was my mother. This special is a pretty good size T-bone with mashed and gravy, either fresh baked bread or cornbread. And whatever you want to drank. That's $2.50"

"That's what I'll have, thank you." Matt said. "How about you Ranger can I buy you some supper?"

Ben studied for just a minute and then said, "It's a little early for me, but what the hell, bring me the same thing "

The conversation flowed freely after that. Matt got into fine details about what he planned to grow on his 200 acres. He talked about how he wanted maybe 30 head of cattle, some hogs and enough chickens to keep a steady supply of eggs. He wanted at least two milk cows. And he wanted to give him a couple of well-trained border Collies but before he could do any of that, he had to commit himself to building a house with enough bedrooms for at least six children. A bam with at least six or eight stalls in it. Then he planned on raising about 100 acres of cotton. It seemed that there was a good market for cotton being that most clothes were made of it.

Then as far as a while he figures that's going to take some time. Not all women are suited to live and work on a farm, most women want to live in town or at least very close to it.

Then abruptly the conversation changed when Matt ask Ben. "Why aren't you married?"

"Not many women want to be married to a man who puts his life on the line everyday to enforce the law. Women today want a man that's going to be there all the time. Not just once in. So many years ago I made the choice not to get married. Although I have had a few lady friends over the years. But none that I ever got really serious about."

"That's not the kind of life that I want, maybe I'm crazy but, I want a woman that's going to fuss at me when I do something wrong, and is going to love me to death when I do something right I know There's one out there for me. The problem is finding her. Matt said this as he took a good-sized bite of a well-cooked T- bone steak.

Matt and Ben finished their supper and remained there sitting, drinking coffee. And enjoying some good conversation. Both men had lost track of Time and it wasn't Consuela came over to the table and sad , "I'm sorry for disturbing your gentlemen but I'm going to be closing in about 15 minutes and I need to get your table cleaned off."

Startled both men looked at their pocket watches and seen that they had been sitting there talking for almost 5 hours.

Ben was the first one to speak, "Where in the hell did the day go to?

I can't believe we've been sitting here for a little better than five hours. But I must admit that it is one of the most enjoyable days that I have spent in a long time. "Then he looked over at Matt and continued by saying ,"Matt Rivers, I have talked more to you in five hours than I have talked to anybody else in the last 30 days, I do believe that we just may have made the foundation for a mighty strong friendship."

Just about time Marshall Trudeau came through the door with a look of utter disgust. Walking straight over to the table where Ben and Matt sat he pulled out a chair, plopped down in it. He turned and looked at Consuela and said. "Sorry Consuela but we've got business to discuss. I think you better bring us another round of coffee, then almost apologetic he said "please "

Then Trudeau questioningly and ask, "What's up Millard?"

"I know that you were planning to go to Denver and pick up this Klein fellow but I have been instructed by the federal judge in town that because he has to be transported across state lines that the responsibility falls on me. I know the Ben .I don't like it any better than you do, but the judge just said, "Do it!!" So as soon as I can map cut the shortest and fastest way to go I'll be leaving it's going to be a lot easier on horseback then trying to wide a stage. I figure I can cut at least 100 or maybe 1125 miles off of the trip by riding in a straight line."

Then Marshall Trudeau turned to Matt and said, "I understand you're going to be heading to the other side of Denver up in North Park."

Matt shook his head and with a great big grin he answered. "Yes sir I sure am, there are some ranches up there in North Park that are in dire need of people who know how to break horses, without breaking their spent. They really must be hurting because they're praying anywhere between $50 and $100 ahead. I guess it just depends on how much trouble you have"

"When where you planning on leaving?"

I figured my horse could stand at least one more full days rest, I wrote him pretty hard getting here. So, I would say the day after tomorrow at sun up I'll be on my way. When were you planning to leave Marshall?"

There's a few thing I got a take care of in the office so I would say midafternoon tomorrow I'll be headed out I figure I can get in alone or 25 miles before it goes too dark to ride. Maybe we'll meet up somewhere along the trail"

Matt stuck out his hands to the Marshall and said, "maybe so Marshall, maybe so. Oh by the way did you notice that I didn't call you Millard?!!

"Yeah I noticed and if you ever do, I just might shoot you"

Matt was plainly trying to tease the Marshall because he continued talking "Why did the Ranger get by with calling you Millard, and I can't?

"Because he's a ranger, a lawman and a lot faster on the draw and I am?

Matt just looked at Trudeau and said "oh okay, that's a good enough reason"

Consuela walked over to the table and handed Ben a ring of keys and said, "Lockup for me when you are ready to leave, there's a fresh pot of coffee in the kitchen help yourself. I'm going home and go to bed, 4:30 in the morning comes early, and goodnight you'll."

Matt locked over Ben and then said. "Unless I'm crazy, I believe that woman is kind of sweet on you."

Ben simply said, "Like I said, just friends"

"Well it's been real nice Matt but, I got my rounds to make, and I'm already past-due. So I'm going to bid you a goodnight and if I don't see you again before you leave for Colorado., keep the wind and the sun at your back, your six shooter loaded and your eyes on the horizon ,but most of all pay attention to your horses ears. He'll hear things that you don't.

The two men walked out to the restaurant together, and while the ranger locked up for Consuela, Matt made his way over to the hotel and was soon in his bed and sound asleep.

The sounds of El Paso waking up woke Matt, he sat up on the edge of the bed and looked at his watch .It was 5:30 and for someone who doesn't have anything planned for the day. It's kind of early to be get met. But he was up so he might as well go get some breakfast .then he thought he would walk down to the stables and give his horse a good rubdown and some extra cats other than that there was nothing else he needed to do, except to say goodbye to his former employee and all the fellows that he worked with .Everything but the clothes on his back were already in his saddle bags or his bedroll. Maybe it would be a good time to give his 45 in his Winchester a real good cleaning .After all there were still a lot of Indians between El Paso and Denver. Thanks God. Most of them have made peace with the white man.

When Matt walked into the restaurant he was surprise to see Consuela already there and evidently she had brought her oldest daughter with her to help out.

Sitting down at the table Consuela walked over and said I wasn't looking for you this early in the morning. I figured you would sleep in till at least 6:30 Matt looked up at her and with a smile he said "I got hungry"

Consuela just laughed and said "I can fix that, do you want that special this morning?"

"As long as there is a lot of it. Okay"

Matt had just started to eat his breakfast when Trudeau walk through the door. And it look like he had a bad night, He looked over at Consuela and in a rough tone of voice said, "Bring me a whole pot of coffee "

Consuela put her hand in her hips and with a stem look in her eyes she said, don't you think you should finish that sentence Mr. Trudeau!!

Trudeau stopped without taking another step, turn around and said, please!

That's better, "Consuela said as she turned and went into the kitchen.

Turning around and looking over the dining room Trudeau seen Matt and immediately headed over to his table. Stopping before he sat down Trudeau said, "Being ever body is in a bad mood this morning maybe I better ask if I can join you. Well can I?" After taking a sip of his coffee Matt smiled and said, "I don't know, can you?"

Trudeau sat down and after laying his hat in the chair next to him he said, "Matt, I think I must be going crazy, because all night long I had the feeling that someone was following me. I sat quite a few traps last night trying to find out if someone was following me. But evidently I was just paranoid because nothing ever happened. By the way to let me get out of here without an apology to Consuela, and it's got to be loud enough that everyone hears it."

Don't worry. I'll make sure you don't forget." Matt said right before taking a big bite of some fried potatoes and a piece of steak.

Consuela brought a pot of coffee and a cup to the table. He immediately Trudeau stood up and called for everyone's attention. Then he got down on one knees and apologized to Consuela almost as loud as he could talk Everyone applauded but Consuela pointed at him and then put her finger right between his eyes and said "I don't care if you are a United States Marshal, don't you ever talk to me ever like that again and I'll beat you with a bloom.."

After Trudeau had sat back down in the chair. Matt said, "like I said, I do believe that the woman like you, a lot."

Trudeau looked at Matt and only said two words "shut up!"

Most of the people in the restaurant heard what Matt had said and had also heard Trudeau's response. Because everyone started laughing including Consuela. From there on there was a lot of friendly conversation rom everyone in the restaurant. One gentlemen asked Trudeau what he was going to wear at his wedding, that's when Consuela told him," you better shut up too!"

This even made the people laugh harder.

Matt just happened to glance at Consuela's older daughter and she was laughing so hard she had tears running down to her cheeks Trudeau just laid his head over to the table and said "looks like today's going to be a continuance of last night.

Consuela waked over to the table and handed Trudeau a glass with three fingers of whiskey in it and said. "Here makes this with your coffee maybe it will help."

I guess Trudeau didn't want to argue anymore because he stood up and said "thank you for being so kind ma'am"

Matt had finished his breakfast and the pot of coffee that Consuela had brought him so he stood up and told Trudeau. "I think I'll go and save my goodbyes out to Mr. Walters ranch, I'm going to miss working for that man, and with the guys I have really grown quiet fond of everybody on that ranch, But like I've heard you say before, there comes a time when everyone has to move on, after all life is supposed to be one continuous adventure.

With the sun barely brightening up the sky wishing comes well into saddling his home as he had already packed his belongings and any supplies that he would need was a long trip that he was preparing to take. He had been notified by a friend of his in North Park Colorado, which layed between Granby and Walden in North Park. That the Michigan River Ranch needed someone to break and train Appaloosa quarter horses. Matt had just 30 days to make the trip from Abilene Texas to North Park.

Matthew had already said he is goodbye to his bunk mates and the owner of the ranch that he had spent the winter riding fence for it wins a hard decision for Matt to make to leave here because he had work for the past so years for this ranch and he had grown quiet fond of the owner and his family and of course the rest of the Cowboys, After all they were what made this ranch function. So, without looking back Matthew stepped into the saddle and spurred his hammerhead Roan into a gallop.

He figured he would follow the stagecoach trail up toward up to the foothills in Southeastern Colorado and then follow one to the old Indian traits going Northwest straight into Denver. He would follow that trail straight up through Fraser and then when he reached Granby he would turn to North that would lead him directly to the Michigan River Ranch. He figured it would take him approximately 3 weeks to make the trip.

It was not very far to the Oklahoma Panhandle and once he crossed that he would be in South-Central Colorado. By cutting northwest he would save himself at least 100 miles. By cutting northwest it was going to be a hard long climb to get up the mountains that would leave him into Denver and then a hard climb to Fraser, once he got to Fraser , the land would level out and be a lot easier covered.

Matt found himself looking forward to the trip because long ago he had made up his mind that he wanted to make enough money to buy him a section of land and start his own ranch, and he wanted to do this East of Sam Antonio there was more green grass and level ground in that area than there was Abilene. By taking this job of breaking and training this Appaloosa quarter horses, he would make enough money to buy that land. The owner of the Michigan River Ranch had 600 horses to break and train and he was paying 510 a horse. Matthew figure that it would take him at the very least the entire summer to break all of these horses and that meant working from sun up to sun down. Seven days a week, Matthew was 28 years old and he weighed at about 190 pound. He stood 6 foot three and was not afraid to work. So there was still time for him to make his money and get his ranch.

The next few days were spent at an easy peace going through the top hat of Texas and Panhandle Oklahoma. Mainly because it was pretty much dessert where water was hard to find the only place there was to find water was at a relay station that had been set up by the Overland stage company.

They usually set these relay stations up every 20 to 25 miles that was a good workday for stagecoach team of horses. So he could stop and water his horses and refill his canteen and his horses could rest. Matthew had found out years ago that the best way, and the best time to travel over the dessert, is at Nights it's cooler and easier on not only the horses but himself.

When the time came when he started entering the foothills of the Rocky Mountains, there would be no problem with water or grass for the horse. There would even be some venison for him but he still had about 160 miles to go before he reached the foothills, so he realized that he must take his time and patience was a necessity, not only for him but for the horses.

He spent his time studying the landscape and looking for any rock formation, or any sign of anything that would could be used as a landmark. Matthew had never traveled the stagecoach trail before, so be needed to familiarize himself with the entire route, Which for Matthew, was a task that he looked forward to, Looking at the scenery and acquiring knowledge that was something that Matthew really enjoyed.

Once a day he would meet the southbound stagecoach, they would stop and talk for a while and swap anything of interest that they might have seen going south, and in turn Matthew would tell them of anything he seen while travelling north. After all there were still a lot of bad men making their own in the Texas and Oklahoma Badlands. This included the southeast tip of Colorado and the Southwestern tip of Kansas.

Matthew knew that when he stopped for the night, if he didn't stop at a relay station, he must not build or have a fire after dark. This was simply because it would be an open invitation to any bad men that were around. He would have to build a fire just big enough to make a pot of coffee and his meal would consist of beef jerky, biscuits and coffee. After eating he would unroll his bedroll and sleep for a few hours which meant that he would be awake around midnight and he would have a good five or six hours of the cool night to ride across the dessert , Usually he could cover at an easy pace about 3 1/2 to 4 miles. At an hour without putting his horses any faster than a good try or even an easy walk.

As the crow flies, it was about 700 miles from Abilene Texas to Denver Colorado so Matthew figured if he covered 30 miles a day it would take him about 25 days to make the trip. That would give him and his horses just about a week to rest up before going to work. Breaking these horses was something that Matthew was looking forward to.

CPSIA information can be obtained
at www.ICGtesting.com
Printed in the USA
BVHW071355141220
595676BV00001B/174

9 781647 492717